GREENSHIFT

BY

HEIDI RUBY MILLER

DOG STAR
BOOKS

GREENSHIFT © 2013
by Heidi Ruby Miller

Published by Dog Star Books
Bowie, MD

First Edition

Cover Image: Bradley Sharp
Book Design: Jeremy Zerfoss

Printed in the United States of America

ISBN: 978-1-935738-54-1

Library of Congress Control Number: 2013949323

www.DogStarBooks.net

For Jason—You know I see an
Armadan when I look at you, right?

ACKNOWLEDGMENTS

Thank you to Jennifer Barnes, Michael Duff, Diane Turnshek, Jason Jack Miller, and Sharon Ruby. You helped me give life to this latest tale in the Ambasadora-verse.

Thank you to Dana Marton for not only writing the foreword to this book, but for being a supportive friend and peer. So glad we met at Seton Hill way back when!

Thank you to all the fans of the Ambasadora series. Your excitement about my science fictional world and the people who live there keeps me dreaming up new plots and new stories to share.

FOREWORD

By Dana Marton

When an author writes an action adventure thriller, even one that takes place in another universe, it helps if she's an action adventure heroine herself, which Heidi Ruby Miller most certainly is. I had the honor of attending Seton Hill University's Writing Popular Fiction graduate program with her, and I couldn't be more thrilled for the amazing career she's had in publishing since. She's a world traveler, a nuanced writer, an exceptional editor—someone I explicitly trust when I pick up one of her books. Her experience with foreign languages and travel, with archeology and geography give the invisible foundation to her stories. Reading them is an authentic experience.

Fans of the first book in the main *Ambasadora* series, *Marked by Light*, will be delighted to return to their favorite far-future universe, and those new to Heidi's writing are in for a thrill ride, able to start with *Greenshift*, a romantic prequel that is a standalone story within the Ambasadora-verse. And then they'll want to go back for another visit again and again.

An ex-warship captain, David Anlow, meets his match in Mari, a young botanist whose genetic uniqueness puts her into the path of a psychopath. When Mari is kidnapped, David will do anything to track her down and save her. This fast pace interplanetary thriller starts out at the top of the roller coaster ride and never slows down. The action and romance are seamlessly woven together, transporting us and leaving us petulant for more when the story is over. I look forward to *Starrie*, the romantic follow-up to *Greenshift* and to *Scarred by Light*, the next book in the main series. Dog Star's motto is: Science Fiction that Goes for the Throat. Heidi has certainly done that with this story and more because *Greenshift* goes for the heart.

--

Dana Marton is the national bestselling author of over 30 novels, including the #1 Kindle fantasy bestseller *The Third Scroll*. She's a Rita Award nominee and the recipient of the Daphne du Maurier Award of Excellence. You can find out more about her at **www.danamarton.com** or on Facebook **www.facebook.com/danamarton**

1

I'm giving you one more chance.

"Unidentified transport vessel, this is Captain David Anlow of the *Argo Protector*. You have entered forbidden space above an embargoed planet. Disengage your weapons or we will take this as a sign of aggression and release gunships. Do you acknowledge?"

The UTV's silence mimicked their response to the first two hails.

David's gunship crews were standing by for launch. Normally he would simply fire a warning shot across the UTV's bow. The sight of a blue-white plasma ball rapidly filling the viewscreen was enough to force even the most powerfully equipped ships to surrender. And the mid-sized transport vessel facing off with them now only had low grade weaponry that would simply vaporize as it glanced off the *Protector's* massive shields.

But David couldn't risk a warning shot here without the plasma punching through the atmosphere of Tampa One and hitting the planet. The sharp silhouette of the oblong UTV was black against the green and white haze of Tampa One. He hadn't been on the pristine planet in decades—few had since Sovereign Prollixer and the Quorum of Archivists designated it an eco sanctuary. That meant no new settlements, no harvesting or mining, only tourists who could pay the exorbitant prices that the Embassy-sanctioned outfitters demanded.

"Third hail," Commander Lyra Simpra said, her cinnamon breath reminding David of his unfinished cup of chai from this morning. "Gunships are a go, Captain."

Lyra had never been a patient woman.

His patience wore thin, too. "Launch gunships two and four."

Still....

The situation *felt wrong* to David. He had been captaining the *Protector* for ten years and had moved rapidly through fleet ranks since enlisting as a teenager. In all that time he learned to hone his instincts. Right now they told him there was something he was missing.

To the gunships he instructed, "Close half the distance. Wait for my order to engage." Then so that only his commander could hear, "Lyra, something feels off about this ship."

"Aside from their outdated registration, non-existent transponder codes, and unwillingness to answer us?" the blonde Armadan asked. "Oh, and there's the bit about their weapons being online."

Only Lyra could get away with talking to him like that, and not just because of how they spent their time together off the bridge. He valued her opinion—she never let emotion cloud her judgment, even when it came to him.

"Do you really think it's a coincidence," she said, "that the day the Embassy sends down the quorum to reconsider the Archenzon embargo, this UTV shows up?"

"Why would they do this?" David asked. "They had to know they'd be hopelessly outgunned."

"Desperation. To make a statement." Lyra didn't sound like she cared about motive. Her mood had been irascible since she returned from a meeting at fleet headquarters last week. She'd never told David what that meeting was about, and he never asked because there would always be parts of their lives they didn't discuss—their positions as officers wouldn't allow it.

Considering their conversation before she attended that meeting, David suspected Lyra had requested a transfer. He shouldn't have brought up marriage again.

The comm officer interrupted his thoughts. "They're responding, sir."

"Argo Protector *we have families on board traveling from Tampa Three. We're requesting an emergency landing. Don't fire.*"

"Convenient," Lyra said.

David agreed. "Why are your weapons online?"

"That can't be. Our ship isn't armed." The man's voice sounded nervous, not necessarily like he was lying, more like the pronouncement caught him unawares.

David looked to his petty officer for confirmation.

"Still reading as online, sir."

"Our sensors report your weapons *are* online. Disengage and we can discuss your emergency situation," David said.

To his comm officer he said, "Relay this information, including the request for an emergency landing, to HQ."

"Yes, sir."

"I'm telling you we don't have any weapons, online or otherwise." Panic infused the man's voice.

"We're assessing your situation now," David said.

"Response coming in from fleet HQ, Captain," the comm officer said.

"Put it through."

"Why hasn't that ship been dealt with?" To David's surprise, he recognized the voice as Rear Admiral Quartis. He expected a comm officer to relay the message. The Embassy must really be concerned with the security for the quorum's little foray on-planet. Most likely the escalating terrorist attacks by the fragger organization this past week.

"Sir, there may be civilian families on board—"

"Squatters, you mean," Quartis snapped back. *"Trying to stake a claim to land on Tampa One before the embargo lifts."*

David had considered that. Debates consumed the Media feeds concerning the upcoming vote that would decide whether those citizens already living on the surface of Tampa One could remain. The single point all legislators agreed upon, however, was that no new immigrants would be tolerated. If the passengers in the UTV were Lower Caste citizens from the ill-formed and dirty world of Tampa Three, David could understand their desire to live in paradise on the rustic and isolated Tampa One.

"I'll have troopers from one of the gunships board them," he said, "and assess the situation from that end. If there's no threat to the *Protector*, the UTV can handle its emergency in our docking bay." To the comm officer David said, "Relay that order to gunship two."

"If that ship doesn't comply with boarding, engage and destroy. The Enforcer is on its way to back you up," Quartis said.

David bristled. "I think one battleship can handle a UTV, sir."

"Don't forget who you're talking to, Captain Anlow."

"You might want to hold your tongue, Captain, before you make us all look bad," Lyra spit out through gritted teeth.

"And, you might want to hold yours, Commander." He didn't need Lyra's pissy attitude right now.

"The UTV's weapons went offline," the petty officer said. "Sir, it's making a break for Tampa One's atmosphere."

"Tell gunships to follow," David said. "Do not engage. Hail the UTV again."

"That goes against direct orders, sir," Lyra said.

"It isn't protocol to shoot down a civilian ship with its weapons offline," David said.

Every trooper on the bridge remained still, listening to the stand-off between the officers.

"Rear Admiral Quartis's direct order overrides fleet protocol according to Section 4.30-74 of the Armadan—"

David cut Lyra off. "I'm not blasting a passenger transport out of the sky without true proof of threat. You may return to your quarters, Commander Simpra."

"I'm afraid I can't do that, David."

His head snapped around at the use of his given name. That should have been the biggest surprise, but it paled in comparison to the shock of seeing her pointing a cender between his eyes.

"This isn't personal," she said.

"Gunships standing by—Sir, gunships from the *Enforcer* just fired on the UTV."

David watched the wall-sized viewscreen as the UTV broke apart into hundreds of red-orange fireballs plunging through Tampa One's atmosphere.

The sub-orbital ship's gangway dropped slowly, first revealing stark white clouds mushrooming into a deep blue sky then the undulating surface of a brilliant turquoise sea on Tampa Deux. Wren had never seen anything like this back on Deleine, even along the coast of the Chac Territory where the ocean wasn't quite as polluted as the rest of the planet. And it smelled just as she had imagined, like a thousand air purifiers were working at once.

She could never leave this beautiful place…because she was probably going to die here.

Terror seized her again, freezing her feet to the dock. Wren's heart pounded so hard, and the blood pushed through her veins with such force, that she thought she might pass out.

"Please don't do this," she begged Carlos, the tall blonde Armadan who pulled her along the private dock. His large hand completely wrapped around her bicep, ensuring she went only where he intended. Not that he would help her anyway—he was only hired muscle with no authority to do anything except what Dale Zapona told him to.

She implored Dale. "Please. I want to go home. You can't sell me."

The wealthy business mogul ignored her pleas.

"You said you would show me the system." Her voice elevated in panic and outrage, wishing she had refused his offer of adventure back at the mining consortium headquarters on Deleine. Sitting behind a desk all day and reviewing miners' health benefits didn't seem so bad. "You lied about everything." She despised the memories she had of mooning over this man whose secret trade was human trafficking.

"Shut her up," Dale said.

Carlos pulled Wren up close to his chest. "You want me to remind you how rough I can be?"

She still wouldn't have known her fate had Carlos not become bored during the journey and decided to make her his entertainment. He couldn't seem to get it up until he saw her fear. Telling her Dale had made a deal with some psychopath for her enslavement was enough to bring on the terror.

She had been afraid every second of every hour since.

They crossed the synthstone dock over the sea as it became a boardwalk spanning a high dune. Her shoulder length hair curled up and stuck to her neck, and the humid air invited biting insects. Wren swatted at the winged attackers, but they were fast and raised red welts on the fair skin of her exposed arms and legs and where her sleeveless sheath had ripped during her struggle with Carlos back on board the freighter. Her bulging lower lip also bore the evidence of that one and only escape attempt when she had gone mad with the thought of him touching her again.

Carlos promised Liu Stavros would be worse, but the man waiting for them on the exquisite white patio was unexpected.

He was in his early twenties, she guessed, not much older than she was. And very good-looking, reminding her of the guys she and her friends drooled over on the Media feeds from clubs at the Hub and the few exclusive franchises on Deleine.

When he saw them, he spread his arms and asked, "What the hell is this?"

The pink shirt he wore billowed open where he hadn't bothered to button it in the front, revealing a thin, but toned chest and abdomen. She couldn't see any tan lines where the bronze skin disappeared beneath the waistband of his beige linen pants.

He flipped his dark shades up from his boyish button nose to look Wren up and down with light brown eyes—the same shade her eyes used to be until the vaccine turned them golden-orange.

"Where's the blonde?" he asked. "And what's up with the busted lip? You know I won't pay full price for damaged goods."

"She had a little fall," Dale said, though he gave Carlos a look that said the difference in price was coming out of his cut.

"That a fact?" Liu said, unconvinced. "You're lucky if I pay half because I already have one with chestnut hair in there." He hitched a thumb over his shoulder toward the double glass patio doors.

If Wren wasn't what he wanted, maybe they'd let her go. A small hope swam to the top of her fear.

The sick smile that spread across Liu's mouth immediately sank her hope.

"But I guess you did come all this way." A crazed expression warped his handsome features and a fast excitement infused his voice. "The mind minstrel's probing the other one right now." He let the double entendre linger in the air before asking, "Want to hear the music we're making? I just got this thing last week. It cost more than that piece of shit shuttle you landed in. Got it from some Lower Caste kid who claimed he was a fragger. But if his scrawny ass was some anti-Embassy rebel, then I'm the fucking Sovereign."

Dale seemed unimpressed. "I don't need to hear anything and I don't need to see anything. I just need my money, Liu."

"Oh. Come on. You know you want to see it. I know *she's* never seen one in action before." Liu walked over and grabbed Wren's chin roughly in his hand and stared into her eyes, or rather stared *at* them. She was used to people showing a mild interest in her rare genetic defect, but this man studied her irises as though he were a doctor… or some kind of mad scientist.

"How about it?" he asked. "They have any mind minstrels on that cesspool planet you're from?"

She didn't want to answer, didn't want to speak to him or even look at him. So she closed her eyes. His grip on her jaw and chin tightened as he shook her head and forced her to stare back at him. "I asked you a question. Do they have any mind minstrels on that cesspool planet you're from?"

"No."

"Then you're really going to enjoy this." He snagged her forearm and dragged her to the patio doors. She couldn't see anything but the sea and sky reflected in the dark glass, but she could hear muffled music and voices from somewhere inside.

The cacophony of screamed lyrics and erratic beats blasted out at them as soon as Liu ripped open the door.

All Wren could make out at first was a triangle of light piercing into the darkness from the doorway. Then movement caught her attention near the ceiling. A small, thin parallelogram bobbed around as if in a lazy current and shined a strobing beam of blue-green light down onto the bed like a search beacon. Its focus was a rounded lump, secured by leather straps and huddled on one corner of the disheveled sheets.

Liu shouted over the deafening music. "Emotions drive the song, and it'll pick up bits of conversation."

As if to emphasize his point, an eerie strain of "Pick it up, p-p-pick it up," grated along with the fast tempo, repeating until it was nothing more than a manic scream.

Wren's entire body shook from the surreal scene and the sensory overload.

The primal shrieking only excited Liu. He threw his head back, spread his arms and bounced to the sickening beat. "I swear it's reading her fucking mind sometimes." Liu pointed to the lump on the bed and slapped Dale on the shoulder. "The shit it spits out in the lyrics is genius."

Dale's jaw twitched in agitation, and Carlos's skin looked grey in the strobing afterglow of the mind minstrel's light.

Wren wished her sight had never adjusted to the darkened room when the naked woman on the bed twisted around in her leather bindings to face them. Her mouth gaped but no words came out. Dark stains dripped down her jaw and....

Wren followed the trail of drying blood up past the woman's nose.

She should have never looked.

Then she wouldn't have seen the empty sockets.

Liu smiled as he pointed two fingers at Wren's eyes and shouted. "Let's see what kind of music you make."

It had been such a beautiful day.

Only to be ruined by the two contractors strutting down the boardwalk toward David and the *Bard*.

Granted, the morning wasn't perfect—he'd spent most of it negotiating for this berth space at Shiraz Dock, the center of the universe so far as the system was concerned. Then he had to attend a special Embassy meeting, where a bored official wearing a drab grey sheath dress and a tight hair bun informed him that the ship he'd been piloting for only a month would be gaining a new passenger soon. *Sara someone,* an ambasadora. She was part of the new Face of the Embassy program, which was supposed to spread the government's message of goodwill and cheer throughout the six planets.

Why they wanted the *Bard*, a small pleasure cruiser that had been overhauled into a boutique science vessel, to carry a diplomat was never made clear. Not that the Embassy official who had briefed them worried about the many questions David and the other pilots asked. The Embassy owned their ships, so why should they be privy to too many details?

The whole brush-off left David a little pissy. When he had been a fleet captain in the Armada, *he* was the one who decided who should know what...and he was important enough to be trusted with details. That thought had played through his head the entire meeting until it made him regret his decision to take an early—*very early*—retirement.

But as the afternoon stretched onward and David fell into the physicality of unloading the last of their supplies for the *Bard*, he regained his calm and was enjoying the buzz of Hub activity.

And Mari's smile.

The young botanist with red-tipped blonde hair and a tight little body also lived on the *Bard*. Like David, she seemed delighted by Shiraz, where space traffic met water traffic around the expanse of Carrey Bay. The best restaurants in the system were here, too. He considered asking Mari to dinner tonight, enjoying the coolness of evening on one of the patios. Every eatery had a patio because year-round this territory remained sunny and temperate so close to the ocean.

David expected the sun to hide, however, as a cloud of agitation followed the two contractors into the area.

"I'll be back in a minute." He left Mari and Sean, the ship's mech tech, to handle the final pallet of supplies while he met the black-clad members of the Embassy's policing force farther up the boardwalk.

The man on the left David recognized as Killian Doje because of the extra cender strapped to his thigh—as though just two of the incendiary pistols couldn't obliterate a crowd of people when dialed up to full energy.

But David wasn't worried...yet. Technically he was using the berth with the dockmaster's permission, though the bottle of Koley's bourbon David had given the official might not be sufficient incentive for him to stay on David's side when push came to shove. And knowing Killian, there would be a little shoving.

Killian and David's brother, Ben, had had a run-in last year at a bar here at the Hub. What was the name of that overpriced dive? The Atlas or Atlatl or something that started with *At*. Though David had been there when Ben and Killian went at it, and eventually jumped in by his brother's side, the likelihood of the contractor remembering him was remote.

David could stave off this confrontation a bit longer by making them come knocking at the ship's gangway, but he'd rather meet them halfway than invite trouble into his home. Though he still hadn't settled into the idea that this pleasure cruiser turned science vessel was *home*. Maybe in another few weeks.

"Anlow, how's your brother? Did he jump ship, too?" Killian's voice rang out smooth and confident. "Or were you the only one to abandon the fleet?"

The fleet jab got under David's skin—his retirement had only gone through a few months ago and he still had a fair share of adjusting to do.

"I didn't think you'd remember me. Guess you do have a brain somewhere in that soft head of yours."

Must have seen my name on the entry request. That meant this was a personal vendetta and not an Embassy affair, which worked to David's advantage. He could take on a couple of grudge-carrying contractors, but not formal charges of trespassing.

"This isn't your berth," Killian said.

"You can have it back when we're done."

"Move your ship."

"When I'm ready."

The other contractor with Killian put a hand to one of his cenders. He looked a few years younger than Killian. Probably on a training run and jumpy as a cornered cat. Though David knew Killian had enough sense not to draw in public unless under a bodily threat, he couldn't be sure of the young protégé. Many Armadans underestimated contractors—David didn't. They might not have as much bulk, but their martial arts training gave them a powerful punch. And they had Embassy law on their side.

"Ward." Killian shot a warning look at his charge.

"You back on babysitting duty, Killian? Thought the Embassy would have promoted you by now. Didn't you have a *boot* stepping on your heels that night my brother kicked your ass?"

David looked at Ward to see if the derogatory slur for rookie hit the mark. The twitch in his jaw said it did.

"You're lucky to have this guy," David continued, speaking to Ward. "When my brother started wailing on that other *boot*, Killian jumped right in and took a beating alongside him."

"No one takes a beating for *me*." Ward clamped both hands on the grips of his cenders.

Contractors and their guns. They were like an extra appendage for most. And this particular contractor was playing David's game perfectly. If he could wind Ward up— and not get shot in the process—Killian would have a wild recruit on his hands and leave David and the *Bard* to their own devices.

"Yeah, that's what the other guy said." David gave Ward a dismissive once-over. "But that wasn't what set my brother off. Come to think of it, I can't even remember what the fuss was all about that night. Do *you* remember why we beat the shit out of you, Killian?" David asked.

Killian's hands moved to his cenders.

So maybe David had gone a little too far.

"David's a better pilot than our last guy," Mari said, gripping the handle of a knife from the ship's galley. She'd been nervously trying to engage Sean in conversation since David left to confront the contractors. From the bottom of the *Bard's* covered chartreuse gangway they watched the testosterone levels rising from forty meters away. Her stomach flip-flopped when David raised his voice.

"Don't you think so? That he's a good pilot?" Mari prompted again. Talking was the only way to hide her anxiety. A trait she had honed as a child and brought with her into adulthood. She even talked to herself or *thought out loud* if no one else was around.

The glare from the surrounding waters of Carrey Bay and the heat shimmering from the dark grey concrete stamped in the shape of a real wooden boardwalk gave the scene the appearance of being filtered through glass. But unlike staring from behind a closed window, Mari could experience the world of Tampa Quad's largest dock all around her.

The boats blasted their horns and spaceship engines screeched and boomed overhead. And the smells…. She enjoyed the aromas from restaurant row across the way, but the berth itself smelled stale. Spilled fuel and exhaust from a faulty filter system mixed with the fishiness of the bay at low tide. At least Sean smelled good. His earthy scentbots brought a hint of freshness as he stepped closer to her to get a better view of David and the contractors.

"I know you didn't like the last guy," Mari said. "Neither did I."

She sucked in a breath when one of the contractors closed in.

"Because he wouldn't flirt with you?" Sean's deep voice remained even, but his focus stayed riveted to David's confrontation.

"Who?" Mari asked, trying to loosen the death grip she had on the knife.

"The last pilot."

"Oh," she said.

Sean was humoring her. And she would let him because her stomach was in knots.

"You won't flirt with me either, and I still like you. At least most of the time. You'd think after eight months of living together, you'd be a little more open."

"We share space on the *Bard*," Sean corrected. "We don't live together."

"Same thing. And that's exactly the kind of remark I would expect from someone who hides behind walls and won't even engage in harmless innuendo."

"I'm not the flirting type," Sean said in a half-hearted response.

"No kidding."

Even after they kissed that time he hadn't made any advances toward her. And that was too bad because it was a good kiss. She studied Sean's thin lips as she thought about it. As usual, dark blonde stubble encircled his mouth and edged up his jaw and down his chin to his neck. In fact, she had never seen him clean-shaven. David always shaved, kept himself well-groomed in general, even his clothes were always crisp and fresh, not like the rumpled workers' pants and faded blue cotton tee Sean wore.

Mari had been making comparisons between the two men since David walked on board a few weeks ago. Sean was the guy she used to want, but now all she thought about was David Anlow. He'd even taken the place of Sean as her best friend aboard ship. Because David always cared about what she had to say—and she usually had *a lot* to say.

She bent down to cut the thick plastic that was vacuum-sealed over the final pallet of food supplies delivered that morning. But her attention kept flickering back to David. He had come to their rescue and now paid the price. Down to crackers and crumbs after the Embassy delayed their supply run by two weeks because a fire destroyed a third of Shiraz's berths, David finagled this spot. Apparently the contractors had taken exception to him *borrowing* a berth space.

Standing a head and a half taller than the men squaring off around him, David Anlow dominated the scene in simple navy blue fatigues and a grey t-shirt with the fleet insignia of six globes arching around the silhouettes of crossed battle rifles. His hands rested on his hips, highlighting the broadness of his shoulders. The contractors' hands hovered near the weapons strapped to their thighs. That unnerved her.

"David's not the flirting type either," she said, picking back up on her conversation with Sean in an attempt to lighten her anxiety. It was a half-truth because David never engaged in questionable chitchat with her in front of the others, but he was finally warming up to her when they were alone.

"He was an officer in the fleet," she continued. "They have a certain propriety."

"Hmm," Sean said.

He always knew how to irritate her.

"I'm learning a lot from him," she said. "He's teaching me how to co-pilot the ship. David says all the crew should know how, just in case."

"We're not crew, we're passengers," Sean said. "And you're the only one he's giving private lessons to."

"Maybe he's just being nice to me. Did you ever think of that?" She would admit that David's good-natured jokes held some innuendo, though always safely ambiguous, and he found reasons to touch her almost constantly when they were alone. Innocent little brushes of her hair or a hand at her elbow, but even the casual touches lingered. Of course, she made sure to invent excuses to see him as often as possible.

"I can tell how nice he wants to be by the way he looks at you," Sean said.

That remark made Mari's skin tingle. She couldn't tell if Sean was teasing her or being honest. If she didn't know him better, she'd think the comment came from jealousy, but that wasn't in Sean's nature.

As for David giving her appraising stares, she'd noticed all right. But Mari noticed *everything* David Anlow did—how his pupils dilated when their gazes met, how his body language was always open and inviting, all the signals they were taught to be aware of when seeking a partner. Granted, she may not have taken the advanced classes in courtship and coupling at school, but she knew enough to tell when a man was interested. That's how she knew Sean wasn't.

For Mari, however, her attraction to David went beyond his obvious physical attributes. It was also the fascination of meeting an actual Armadan captain—well, retired captain.

"Why did David quit the fleet so early?" she asked. "In the past three weeks I've heard all about his four brothers, his sister, even his parents and their family estate in the Koley Mountains on Yurai, but he always keeps quiet about his time in the fleet."

"I'll ask him next time we sit down for a beer together."

Sean's sarcasm dropped heavy like Mari's stomach when she watched two more contractors, a male and a female, pop out of the stone and glass security kiosk a dozen meters from David.

She pulled in a deep, nervous breath, filling her nose with Sean's clean scent. David didn't have scentbots, but like the other Armadan who lived aboard the *Bard*, David's skin had a natural, subtle scent that reminded her of green tea leaves. She'd do anything to have him close enough to smell right now and far away from the threatening contractors.

"You should be nicer, a little more respectful," she chided Sean, but her speech was slow and pitchy, no longer able to hide her apprehension.

"Why?" Sean asked. "Because he's my elder?"

She thought she caught a twitch at the edge of Sean's mouth. So maybe he *was* teasing her, trying to take her mind off the escalating scene in front of them.

"*Because*," she said. "He convinced the dockmaster to give us a berth space even though Shiraz wanted to put us off for another week."

Sean remained unimpressed.

"We could have starved."

"We wouldn't have starved," Sean said in that exasperated tone that said his patience grew thin.

She knew he was right, considering the number of small docks within a few hours' ride via a terrestrial or aquatic transport. But she had a penchant for drama thanks to so many obsessive hours watching vids on the Media during a childhood stuck on Deleine.

"Well, we would have had to shuttle all this stuff hundreds of kilometers. Or buy all new supplies, and some of us don't have a lot of money to spare."

Sean didn't say anything to that, having spotted her for the rent on her suite for the second month in a row.

"Besides, this berth is nice," she said. "So close to the Hub activity that we don't even need to take a transport or monorail to be in the middle of it all. It's just a walk or a ferry ride away."

Then she added, "By the way, David's just a little older than you." Which was a stretch because Sean was around thirty or thirty-five or something, and David's formal Embassy bio put him four months shy of sixty, though most people wouldn't have guessed it by looking at him.

"Try twice as old as me."

"He's not even middle age, and have you seen him with his shirt off?"

Sean's expression said that that was the last thing he was thinking about.

"I guess his physique is an inherited Armadan trait." She couldn't stop the volley of nervous words coming out of her mouth. "We didn't have any Armadans around where I grew up. Geir was the first Armadan I ever met, although he isn't as muscled as David, so maybe it's the military training. Do you know why Geir became a scientist instead of joining the fleet? That's more of a Socialite job. I never wondered about that until David came on board…."

Sean's posture tensed as the latest arrivals strode closer to David.

"I know you're itching to be in on this fight," Mari said. "Why don't you go over there? David would probably appreciate the back up." Though maybe he didn't need any just yet, the way the contractors stayed out of his reach.

When David raised his voice and an arm in objection to something the closest man said to him, all four contractors casually pulled their cenders from their thigh holsters and held the weapons at their sides.

Mari nudged Sean's arm. "Okay, you really should go over."

"One more person in the mix won't be good for anyone. Besides, David knows they won't fire their cenders," Sean said.

"How does he know that? How do *you* know that?"

"Too many voyeurs hanging around and taking in the action." Sean gestured to the half dozen small floating balls of telescoping cameras and directional microphones that gathered in a circle above the uneasy scene.

A white gull attempted to land on one voyeur, which had been hovering patiently over the area, but the bird thought better of it when two cameras extended from the voyeur in a fast snap.

Giant Media screens perched above the docks from well-positioned kiosks picked up the live feed and broadcasted the confrontation for not only those within the immediate vicinity, but also on several channels across the system. Had Mari's family been tuned into these particular channels out of the millions available, they would be able to see the man she was so enthralled with—dark hair, prominent jawline, and long legs extending from a perfect backside.

When David forced one of the contractors to back up ever so slightly, Mari's heart beat a little faster. His confidence amazed her. She wanted to command control of a situation, any situation, like he did.

Raised voices reached her ears from the scene in front of her the same time they echoed from the nearest Media screen.

"You need to move your ship out now." It was one of the original male contractors speaking. His ebony hair and brows matched his clothing. Like all contractors he was perfectly beautiful with olive skin and icy blue eyes.

The shot switched to David, whose features were more masculine than delicate. *"As soon as we inventory our supplies. I'm thinking that could take a couple of days."* His slight accent came through in the way he pronounced his vowels.

The camera zoomed in on his face. His tan skin stretched over angled planes, though the screen didn't do his eyes justice. They looked like the pale grey of the winter sky back in her home territory, but his irises held a slight tint of deeper blue if you got close enough to notice, and she'd been close enough plenty of times.

"A couple of days?" Sean grumbled. "What the hell is he talking about? I'm not staying here just so he can prove a point. I have stuff to do."

Sean always had *stuff to do*. He had a brilliant mind, especially when it came to the ship's systems and techy gadgets, probably why they called him a mech tech, but Mari believed Sean's intelligence was his biggest enemy. He thought too much and tried to lose himself in his work, or the virtual arena of the V-side, to avoid interacting in the real world. And he hated to be docked here at the Embassy Hub. Mari found it exciting to be in the middle of the busiest city in the system—well, usually.

She was already worried about losing another client this week, adding to her mounting financial problems, and today's situation compounded her nervous energy, yet no one else paid the slightest attention to what was happening. The bustle around Shiraz never slowed for anything.

Another exchange between David and the contractors played on the Media screens. Among the frenzied music dubbed over the scene to add excitement, Mari heard David say, "*The way you're stroking that piece makes me think Killian here should be watching his ass.*"

The contractor leveled his pistol at David. Mari's mouth went dry.

David ignored the cender and stuck his finger in the younger guy's chest, bending down to face him. His voice echoed from screen to screen. "*You keep pointing that weapon at me and I'll show you how to use it.*"

Mari's focus bounced from David and the contractor to their images augmented on the Media screens like she watched a pair of athletes volleying serves. She missed whatever David said next, but suddenly all but one contractor had a gun pointed at him.

Sean snagged the knife from Mari's hand and tucked it discreetly against his side as he walked down the boardwalk toward the action.

That pissed them off.

David's verbal sparring with the armed group had taken a turn for the worse. Maybe he shouldn't have used the word *inbred*, but contractors did like to keep it within the family. It would have been a good insult even if the voyeurs hadn't broadcasted it loud and clear for the whole system to hear. He could have thrown in illegal gene manipulation, but that would have just been petty.

"Don't get me wrong," David said, raising his hands in front of him as though he meant no offense. "It's a good look, a little cold, like your personalities, but pretty."

Killian motioned for the others to lower their weapons. "You have half an hour to get that ship out of here."

"If you have that big of a problem with my ship being here, take it up with the dockmaster." David's words snapped through the Media speakers. He didn't let on that hearing his own harsh tone startled him.

Apparently it made the contractors uneasy as well. They were still twitchy because they knew they had no reason to be here. Of course, most contractors he met never missed an opportunity to flaunt their authority over an Armadan, at least those Armadans not in uniform. Even contractors steered clear of any military involvement. David didn't know how or when the cultural tension between Armadans and contractors began, but it had been gaining momentum recently.

The thought gave him pause. He needed to end this before Ward and his friends stopped taking directions from Killian.

Out of the corner of his eye, David caught Sean meandering toward them. The two latecomers noticed, too. Their attention split between David and Sean. As far as Ward was concerned, though, David was the only thing in the world right now.

"I'd tell your crewman to back off," the female contractor said.

David almost smiled, thinking of the string of expletives that would roll out of Sean Cryer's mouth if he heard that comment.

"I wouldn't worry about him. He's a harmless mech tech." Though David suspected Sean could be dangerous, especially if he had been dosing recently.

David leaned in close to Killian and hid his face so the voyeurs wouldn't be able to eavesdrop. "We both know you have a mark against you after that fight last year. The Embassy is going to throw you out of the guild if this incident goes any further. I may not enforce it, but I do know the law and so do all those viewers catching our exchange at home. Is getting back at me really worth your job? Why don't you just take Ward, get him tucked into bed before it gets dark, and relax for the rest of the evening?"

Killian's expression was blank. Contractors gave new meaning to stoicism. "You're bordering on harassment, Anlow."

"I can keep on my side of the fence," David said. "Can Ward?"

They both knew the answer to that question. Ward bristled for a fight, and Killian couldn't afford for that to happen in plain view of the system.

David made a motion for Sean to hang back a bit. To David's surprise, Sean did.

Killian took a moment longer to regard both men before smacking his shoulder into David's chest as he pushed past. "I'd watch my back if I were you. These docks can be dangerous."

The other contractors followed Killian's lead, all except for Ward, who flexed his fingers around the grips of his guns and stared at David.

"Let's go, Ward," Killian called to him.

David stood his ground and didn't take his eyes off the group.

Sean sidled up beside him, not speaking until the four contractors slipped back inside the security kiosk. "What the hell was that all about?"

"They just wanted to say hi."

"We're not staying here a couple of days," Sean said. "We have to pick up Geir."

David's appreciation for Sean backing him up evaporated.

"Geir's sitting tight until the end of the week."

"We're not staying here," Sean repeated as they walked down the boardwalk.

"I think that's a decision to be made by everyone," David said. "I know Kenon and Soli asked if it would be possible to spend a little more time with their amours. And Mari likes any excuse to be off-ship. I guess that leaves you with the only dissenting vote."

"Do you think they'd vote that way if they knew this was all just an opportunity for you to dick over those contractors?"

David ignored Sean as they neared the *Bard*. Mari's gaze met them. Even with David standing lower than her on the sloping gangway, she still had to look up at him slightly. She lightened his mood considerably. "This the last one?" he asked.

"Last one," she said.

David gave her a fast once over, lingering on the bit of leg peeking between her short skirt and thigh high boots. He quickly diverted his attention to her face. "We're going to stay the night."

25

"Soli will be happy to spend some extra time with Trala, especially since they're expecting," Mari said. "And Kenon won't have to leave Giselle so soon. She's his prime. Have you ever seen her? She's blonde and beautiful. A little snobbish, but Kenon doesn't seem to notice. Of course he has three amours total so when he gets sick of one he visits the others. Maybe he'll pop over to see them all before we go."

The excitement in Mari's face as she talked about the people in her life made David happy.

"This will be fun, Sean, won't it?" she asked.

"Not so much." He passed Mari on the gangway to head back inside.

"Sean." Mari pointed to the final food pallet. " Supplies?"

Sean said over his shoulder, "I vote David unloads it."

"He's always so pleasant," David said.

"Really Sean's a good guy. He just has to get used to you."

"I've been here almost a month."

"A month's not long enough for Sean," she said. "Are you hungry? We actually have food on board now. Well, most of it is on board." Mari looked at the pallet waiting to be wheeled up the gangway.

"I'll get that," David said. "Then maybe we could go out for dinner? I know a couple of great restaurants along the bay."

"Yes." Mari barely let David finish. "I'll go change."

She put her palm against his chest in a formal gesture, but the warmth of her hand radiating through his t-shirt didn't inspire thoughts of decorum in David.

"Anyone else coming with us?" she asked, her fingertips moving ever so slightly against the fabric of his shirt. "I think I'll wear that blue and silver dress you said you liked. You remember which one, don't you? I wore it during your first week aboard when we all went out in Steckert City before Geir started his long-term project there. I wonder how Geir is—"

"I remember the dress," David said gently, knowing if he didn't interrupt her now they'd still be standing here at midnight. "And I think it should just be you and me this time."

"Good idea." She brushed her lips against his, bringing the world to a screeching halt in that moment. "Very good idea," she whispered, her face so close to his he could feel her breath dance across his cheek. Her proximity raised the little hairs on the back of his neck in a way even his earlier confrontation couldn't.

"See you in a bit." She pushed away from him and walked up the gangway, but he could hear her pace pick up once she hit the grand staircase in the foyer. He was glad to know she was as excited about tonight as he was.

Civvy life isn't so bad.

From their waterside table at the Rose of Sharon, David watched the synth spiders draw rainbow lines through the night air in time to the music they played. Like orchestral conductors their metallic legs looped and jabbed, weaving swirls of greens and blues then oranges and reds through the darkness above the reflective waters of Carrey Bay. A mosaic of patterned lights fronted luxury hotels in the tourist zone, enticing guests to come and stay or just drop by for a visit to shop and dine.

Shiraz Dock came alive at night, the officious Hub traffic from the day transforming into glittery party-goers. David, sporting civilian dress pants and a green button down shirt instead of his fleet uniform, felt like he fit in for once. He didn't realize he would enjoy being a regular citizen again. Several women gave him more than a passing glance, even as they hung on the arms of their escorts for the evening. Normally he would have been flattered, maybe thrown a smile or a wink their way, but tonight his interest never strayed from Boston Maribu. He had only called her by her given name the first time they met. The face she made said she would prefer Mari.

She received more than her share of interest, too, especially in the tiny silver and blue dress which skirted on being a little too immodest for an establishment like the upscale Rose of Sharon. But if she noticed any of the men trying to catch her eye, she never acknowledged them.

"Soli and Kenon live somewhere over there in Wright's Landing." Mari gestured toward the not-so-far shore, whose rolling hills sparkled with glimpses of spotlighted towers and multi-pitched roofs, a welcome-home beacon to those wealthy Hub citizens who could afford the real estate. "Though nowhere near one another. It's a huge place."

"I'm surprised Kenon would be interested in scientific work if his family is so wealthy. He doesn't exactly strike me as the ambitious type," David said, thinking about the foppish man who never really seemed to *do* anything but hang out on the *Bard* and complain about his accommodations.

"I don't think he likes staying on-planet too long. He'd have to be around all his amours then." Mari winked. "At least that's what Soli told me. And if anyone would know, it would be Soli."

David silently agreed. Solimar Robbins was an Embassy-sanctioned archivist, which meant she had a duty to record all events surrounding her for public record. Coming from the privacy of the Armada, David hadn't taken to Soli's busybody nature quite yet, though she continued to be very warm toward him. And she and Mari were close.

"The boats are taking up anchor to view the light show already." Mari looked around with those big, beautiful eyes that always managed to captivate him. They owed their unique coral color to a slight reaction to a childhood vaccine. The effect brought a golden luminosity and intensity to her irises that he had never seen before. From the time he first met her he wanted to see those eyes staring up at him from his bed.

The fact that she seemed game, eager in fact, should have thrilled him, but the more he got to know her through stories of her family and her out-of-the-way home on Deleine, the more she talked about her dreams and hopes for the future, the more *he* wanted to take things slowly, maybe be a part of that future, as foolish as the idea might sound. It took him this long before deciding to ask her out because they had formed a true friendship, and it made him a little nervous to change that dynamic. If things went wrong, not only would they feel awkward around one another every time they passed on the small ship, but he'd lose the closest friend he'd made since retiring.

Yet all he could think about was how their friendship would only make a physical relationship that much more satisfying, how he could easily see spending the rest of his days talking to Mari, seeing life through her eyes.

What the hell is wrong with me?

His thoughts made him feel like a sentimental fool. Maybe his clock was ticking, that biological imperative to find a prime and make some babies. It was a little early to be thinking of marriage and a family, at least by Armadan standards—he had forty good years before he even hit his century mark. But, nonetheless, he was finally feeling that pull that his younger brother, Ben, had been describing for years. Had any of Ben's relationships worked out, he would have been happy to settle down in his twenties, but as he followed David through his fifties, he'd probably just wait until he retired from the fleet.

At a proper age, maybe eighty or ninety, like Dad, not like me who couldn't even stick it out until middle-age.

When David started on this path of regret at having given up his fleet commission, he just remembered the placid, stony look on Lyra's face when she put a gun to his head and challenged his control of the *Argo Protector*. It had been the single most heart-breaking moment in his life.

"Don't you think so?" Mari asked.

David hadn't been paying attention. Taking a fifty/fifty chance, he said, "Yes."

Apparently it was his lucky night because she seemed pleased with his response.

Once again she brought him back to the present and grounded him. She would never know how grateful he was for those times when just the cadence of her voice coaxed him out of that dark place in his head. Just like her beautiful, shining eyes, Mari had become his light.

"Do you remember how you started ordering everyone around your first day on the *Bard*?" she asked.

"And how they all just snickered and walked away? Yeah, I do." David could laugh about it now, but at the time he'd been pissed.

"Except for me," Mari said.

"Except for you," David agreed. "You were always there to help, even when I didn't need it." He smiled to let her know he was joking.

"If you're talking about that time I *accidentally* sent all your clothes to the cleaners and you had to borrow Geir's stuff for two days...."

"That's exactly what I was thinking about."

"You looked good in those tight t-shirts," she said.

The blush that crept into her cheeks made David want to touch her, to see if her skin felt as flushed as it looked.

She got a little shy then and worried her bottom lip between her teeth.

I can do that for you. He was mesmerized by that plump, wet lip.

She stared at him like she knew his thoughts. The blush grew a little deeper. This time she lowered her eyes and moved the food around on her plate with her fork, but she couldn't hide her smile.

She did this often, being bold and forward as though coming on to him, then pulling back demurely at the last second. It drove him crazy...in an absolutely wonderful way.

As they finished up dinner, she talked about each detail surrounding them on the waterside patio. From the Rose of Sharon's iridescent purple and green canopy overhead to the string quartet warming up in the main dining room, she was excited by it all.

Her swooping hand gestures punctuated her enthusiasm and made the matching silver cuffs she wore on her small biceps glitter in the magenta glow of the candlelight. The design of delicate vines weaving around her arms in silvery swirls couldn't have matched her personality better—not just that she liked shiny jewelry and anything that had to do with plants, but because she was so lithe and wispy and easily wove her conversation from one topic to the other. He could imagine her wearing those cuffs and nothing else as he studied the facets of her animated face.

"The gardenias along Wright's Landing will be blooming in a day or two," she said. "They're supposedly an heirloom variety native to here, but I don't believe it. In this climate? They have to be hybridized with a heartier strain, probably gened up in a lab. But it's still breath-taking to see nothing but white flowers stretching all along that side of the bay, and the smell is wonderful."

He couldn't imagine anything smelled better than Mari. Even when she wasn't around him, he swore he still caught a hint of citrus and flowery notes from her scentbots. Maybe the pheromones that those bots also released through her pores were working overtime on him. He envisioned pulling her close and breathing her in, tasting the scent on her lips and every patch of skin.

For most of the evening, he'd avoided looking directly at her perky nipples pushing against the silky fabric of her dress. But now his gaze kept drifting as more racy thoughts swept through his mind, bringing the expected reaction down below. At least there was a dinner table hiding him. He needed to think of something else.

"The gardenias are nice," he said. "I've seen them a couple of times here before. But, I have to say, they pale in comparison to spring in the Koley Mountains.

The rhododendron and laurel bloom the same time as most of the wildflowers. The forest is painted for kilometers in brilliant color. From my lake house, the surrounding mountains look like one of those pixel paintings. Do you remember those? They were popular a few years back."

Mari shook her head no.

So maybe it was more than a few years back.

"They were an odd fad. The artists would only put a dot of color every so often on a solid monochromatic canvas to give the impression of distance."

Mari rested her chin in her hand and looked at David with a lazy, wistful expression. "I'd like to see that. Your lake house, not the paintings. There weren't many lakes where I grew up on Deleine. At least not ones that weren't chemically polluted or had a river of acid mine drainage pouring into them. Do you have a boat?"

"Everyone in the family does. It's the easiest way to get around Cheat Lake."

"I bet it's like paradise. When we studied all the eco-systems on Yurai in school, I always said I'd go there one day. Koley is in the Sparta Territory, isn't it?"

"That's right." He took a sip of scotch. "You would enjoy the mountains. They're the best part of Sparta, or any of the other territories on Yurai, in my opinion."

"Then you should take me there, so I can decide for myself if it's paradise."

He couldn't tell if her smile was genuine or mischievous, but his body took her words as innuendo.

"I'm glad you suggested this place," she said. "I've never eaten here. Or any place this nice. I like the name—the Rose of Sharon. Of course, I like most everything that has to do with flowers and plants."

David liked most everything that had to do with Mari, especially hearing her talk, even if he sometimes got distracted in his own thoughts while she went into an especially long soliloquy.

"Do you know I've never seen a real Rose of Sharon bloom?" she asked. "I mean, on vids, yeah, but you can't smell a vid, can't touch one." She reached out to the dual blossoms branching out of a narrow silver vase in the middle of the table and ran light fingertips over the pink petals.

David nearly felt her caress on his skin. That warm, light feeling in his chest returned, and for once he allowed himself to indulge in it.

So much of life and the world seemed new and fascinating to Mari. She was a born scientist, contemplating the little intricacies that David never stopped to think about.

He could listen to the sound of her voice all night. Its rich tone was soft and feminine like her. Of course, it sounded more like a girl's voice than a woman's, especially when she was excited, but Mari *was* only nineteen. The thought brought a little weight to his lightness, making him ask, *what am I doing?*

His attraction to Mari unsettled him, not necessarily just because of their age difference—Armadan men usually didn't settle down until after their fleet service and therefore had to seek out younger amours, though maybe not *forty years* younger— rather, David feared his captivation with Mari might be a substitute for the *Argo Protector*, the battleship he'd captained for the past decade. An outsider would say so because of David's unplanned retirement, but he remained unconvinced. He genuinely enjoyed being around Mari and not just because she dressed so provocatively and had the little body to back it up. The slinky dress that skimmed the top of her thighs, and had no back to speak of, was a perfect example.

He'd had his share of women over the years, mostly battle maidens, a few Socialites like Mari, but he hadn't considered really getting to know much about any of them.

Lyra was the closest.

Then she betrayed him, though *betrayed* probably wasn't harsh enough for a woman who staged a mutiny on his ship. The fleet eventually released her of all culpability for reasons David was never privy to—a double betrayal.

Lyra was the reason he left the fleet, his duty, and the only life he'd known. Perhaps that was really why David was drawn to Mari—she was *nothing* like Lyra Simpra. He'd decide later if that was a good enough reason to become involved with her. Right now he just wanted the warmth to return. He slid his hand across the table to encircle Mari's. The touch stopped her in mid-sentence and brought her gaze to his.

The server brought another glass of wine for Mari and a third scotch for David. As he pulled his hand away, Mari grabbed it again and said, "I like you, David."

He caught the smile on the server's face as the man pretended not to listen. Mari's sudden proclamation and unabashed honesty, even in front of a stranger, made those warm feelings flame a little hotter inside David. They seemed inappropriate for a former fleet officer, but he had never experienced them before, not even with Lyra, and discovered he liked the sensation.

He waited for the server to depart before responding. "I like you, too."

This small admission felt awkward and exposing. He squeezed her hand before letting it go for the safety of his drink.

"You forgot to say 'Valhalla!'" She held up her glass.

David hadn't expected Mari to know the Armadan funerary toast. "Where did you hear that?"

"I saw it on a vid. What does it mean?"

"Actually, I'm not sure of the word's meaning or origin, only that we normally use it when saying good-bye to fallen comrades."

"Oh," Mari said, lowering her glass a bit.

"How about 'to something new?'" He tapped his tumbler against her wine glass. It could have meant Mari's first time at the Rose of Sharon, but maybe she suspected he toasted to the next step of their relationship. He wanted more than friendship from her, and she was pretty obvious about her intentions toward him, which made her the brave one.

"Boston Maribu?" A man edged up next to her. His fine features, small frame, and saccharin genteel manner marked him a Socialite. As did the over-active scentbots, which smelled like a mixture of musk and smoldering wood. It reminded David of a campfire gone wrong.

Who told him that would be a good combination? David never did understand the vanity behind scentbots, but admitted he couldn't imagine Mari without her being awash in citrusy notes.

"I don't mean to interrupt." The look he gave David said he absolutely did mean to interrupt. "But, I can't believe my luck."

"Chairman Zapona, how are you?" Mari sat straighter when she spoke to the man.

"*Dale.* Please, after all the time we've spent together."

"Then you should know to call me Mari," she said.

"Of course."

Dale took the opportunity to kiss her on the cheek, a gesture much less formal than a peck to the forehead, as was customary in this circumstance, at least as far as David was concerned. He already didn't like Dale. He liked him even less when the man caressed Mari's bare shoulder while he spoke.

"I'm in the market for a hydroponics system. Just purchased another freighter for my mining company. The greenshift has been good for business." He looked at David from the corner of his eye and gave a little pause.

"Congratulations?" David dripped a fair amount of sarcasm into his response. He knew very little about the greenshift movement, only that the Embassy decided interplanetary commerce would benefit from hydroponics upgrades. If a ship didn't have to stop for supplies so often, like the *Bard* did, it could be more efficient.

Dale sniffed. "I don't believe we've had the pleasure."

"Oh, I'm sorry," Mari said. "Dale, this is David Anlow, our ship's new navigational leader. David, this is Dale Zapona."

David gave the chairman a half-nod and received half that in return.

"It's good to hear about your new freighter," Mari said. "Your company is really growing."

"More than I could have ever imagined, dear."

Now he was calling her dear?

David missed the next part of the conversation as he contemplated all the things he wanted to call Dale, *chairman* not making the list. It was only when Dale asked Mari, "Are you still available?" and glanced in David's direction did their exchange suddenly become more interesting.

"Yes." The enthusiastic response brought about an emotion David hadn't dealt with in years. When she looked at him like he would be pleased by the offer, too, he knew Mari had missed Dale's innuendo.

"That's good news," Dale said. "Should we meet tomorrow at my home in Wright's Landing and discuss details?"

"Sure," Mari said. "Unless we can't keep the berth." She looked to David anxiously. "Do you think there will be a problem rescheduling departure?"

He wanted to say that it was a big problem, that they were already pushing their luck with the dockmaster, plus they'd now be two days later for Geir's pick up, but David knew he'd already shot down all of these reasons to leave when Sean presented them earlier. It was like David's own argument was coming back to bite him.

"Not a problem at all," he said.

"Then see you tomorrow, my dear." Dale gave Mari another kiss, this one so close to her lips that David's hand squeezed his glass, ready to smash it into Dale's artificially perfect nose.

"Yeah, see you tomorrow," David said.

Dale's smile dissolved as he left.

Once he was out of earshot, Mari said, "I can't believe it." She tapped her blue-tipped fingernails on the table in an excited cadence. "Just when I needed a new client, an old client shows up with a big project. This work could last me the entire year. What an awesome night, don't you think?"

"Great night," he agreed. *Or had been.*

He threw back his scotch, letting its odd mix of vanilla and leather burn away the image of Dale standing so close to Mari.

David remained distracted through dessert. It wasn't only that he didn't care for sweets or that Mari talked at length about calibrating hydroponics systems in multiple gravity environments—the technical aspects of which zipped right over David's head—what bothered David was how a mining company chairman whom Mari hadn't seen in a year's time seemed more at ease around her than David did.

Granted, he and Mari had only met a little more than three weeks ago, but they had spent *a lot* of time together on the *Bard*. Every meal, long talks in the elegant common rooms of the former pleasure cruiser, the piloting lessons on the bridge....

"Are you going to eat that?" Mari jabbed a fork into the chocolate strawberry layer cake on David's plate.

"It's all yours," he said, still amazed at how much Socialites enjoyed sugar. It was like a drug to them. Much like how alcohol was to most Armadans. He raised a finger to their server across the room for another double shot while Mari finished his cake. He'd been sharing dessert with her since their first dinner together, which was also his first day on the *Bard*. She had been aghast that he could let half a slice of buttermilk pie go to waste so made it her mission to take it off his hands. Ever since, he saved all his sweets for her.

David liked this small part of their history together—what he didn't like was that she had a history with Dale Zapona.

"What was it like working with Dale?" David asked, trying to keep his tone nonchalant.

"Okay. I guess. It was a small project, my first project for hire when I still lived on Deleine."

David enjoyed hearing Mari relive her accomplishment. He listened intently as he absent-mindedly paid the server and guided Mari onto the boardwalk with a hand on her lower back.

"Dale offered me a position back then," she said, "on one of his freighters, to engineer another hydroponics system. That was before the greenshift movement. But my family talked me out of it. Said I was too young. I had just turned eighteen so it's not like I was *that* young."

David looked out over the bay so she couldn't see the grin forming at the corner of his mouth. He observed this attitude in new fleet recruits all the time—they felt that eighteen, or sixteen, were magic numbers into adulthood. At fifty-nine David still didn't feel quite like an adult yet. Maybe that attitude was biased, though, considering Mari was out here living life on her own. He'd gotten a ready-made family and career upon entering the fleet in his teens. Mari was doing it all by herself.

"Anyway, I told Dale I had to pass, cried for a couple of days...." She gave David a quick, embarrassed look as though she hadn't meant to reveal that part. "Then I took some medical classes, hoping that would make me more employable than my botany specialty."

"Did it?" David didn't know she was a trained medic. For her to have studied everything that she had must have taken all her childhood. Then again, her mind was incredible. David had always considered himself smart, or at least clever and strategic, but Mari's knowledge of every subject they discussed amazed him.

"Not really," she said, "but the local mines hired me for a few months as a combination hydroponics specialist-medic."

"You don't find that job description very often," David mused.

"On Deleine lots of people do double duty. Maybe because there are more jobs than people willing to move there," she said, matter-of-factly rather than with resentment. "The mining companies are always trying to keep the work force healthy enough to keep digging. Recently they've been investing in ways to grow food underground so the miners can stay down longer and longer. That was actually what prompted the greenshift since the same research could be adapted for spaceships."

She paused and looked into the distance for a moment, and David thought he saw a sadness flash across her features.

"I don't know who would want to stay down in those dark and filthy mines for too long," she said. "Even if it's just to oversee the equipment."

He had heard growing up on Deleine, Upper Caste or not, was tough. No matter where you went on the planet, except maybe the industrialized cities, the economy centered around colossal mining endeavors, and most citizens there derived their income from the mines in one way or another.

Just when he wanted to ask if she was okay, applause erupted up ahead as three acrobats formed a human tower on top of each other's shoulders. In perfect Mari style, she shrugged off her solemness and joined in the cheering. After the trio tumbled back into separate spots, Mari went right onto her next thought.

"That's how I got my suite on the *Bard*. I saved my money for a deposit, bought lab equipment piece by piece, and decided I could be a work-for-hire scientist while seeing the system. And I was still *eighteen* at the time, so that's how much my family knew." Her eyes opened wider and her entire face nearly glowed with pride in the pronouncement.

"I admire your need for independence," David said. There was a lot he admired about her.

A chilled night breeze, laced with music and laughter, blew along the boardwalk as they approached the docks. David welcomed the coolness on his face, but Mari's slight frame shivered with the ten degree drop in temperature. He wished he'd worn a jacket just so he could make the chivalrous gesture of wrapping it around her.

"If you're cold, we can take the ferry back," he said, glancing toward the string of lights marking the waterway docks.

"No, I like walking." She tried to suppress a little chatter to her teeth. "There's so much to see here, and I like to be right where it's all happening."

He tucked her into his side with an arm around her shoulders, trying to warm her as best as he could. She hugged his waist and leaned her head against his chest. They walked through the buskers and tourists of Shiraz as though being together like this was the most natural of states. Not that being this close to her didn't make his heart beat a little stronger or his pants fit a little tighter—he'd have to be comatose not to respond to her. Still, he marveled at how right it felt to be with her.

A traveling drum quartet parading through stopped foot traffic in the middle of the boardwalk. The men and women, dressed in silver with threads of light shimmering along the fabric's seams, high-stepped while pounding on all sizes and shapes of percussion instruments hanging from harnesses on their shoulders.

As the performers danced past, David watched the delight shining in Mari's face.

"You're beautiful," he said.

The compliment captured her attention, so he took the opportunity to lean down and kiss her. The wonderful citrusy notes of her scentbots mixed with the sweet smell of chocolate and strawberry layer cake and night-blooming water lilies on the edge of the bay. He moved his mouth over hers gently, testing her reaction. She responded a little shyly, barely parting her lips, but her hand slid up his chest to caress his face.

The innocence of the moment impacted David more than he expected. The way she slowly explored his mouth, first with her lips, then small darts with the tip of her tongue revealed how much this pleasant action meant to her. His heart pounded faster with the realization. After all these years, all the women he'd touched, none took the time to enjoy a simple kiss as much as Mari did. He, too, had taken the intimacy for granted until this instant.

The shrill and boom of fireworks filled the night air as if celebrating David and Mari's moment. He felt Mari smile beneath his lips and opened his eyes to see her peeking up at a golden flower of sparks lighting the blue-black sky above them.

"Perfect timing," he said, still pressed against her mouth.

"Perfect," was all she said before slipping back into their kiss, not quite as shyly this time.

Dale called Liu Stavros to confirm his price for a blonde with coral-colored eyes.

"This girl had the full effect of the vaccine. Though not to my taste, her eyes are certainly unique, even compared to the other two women I procured."

"And she's blonde, you say?"

"Sunny blonde with dyed red tips, but that can be cut off if you prefer something more natural."

The low laugh that rumbled through Dale's reporter made his stomach queasy. He knew Liu would want the honor of cutting Mari's hair himself. And it wouldn't stop with her red locks. Liu had a sadistic mind that always found new ways to inflict pain upon his conquests.

Dale tried not to think about the rumors he'd heard regarding Liu's sport with women. Too many horrible details about the rapes and disfiguring torture. But he couldn't ignore the memory of seeing one of Liu's victims for himself. Still bound to the bed, shrieking in her post-coital nakedness, eye sockets empty and bloody. That woman had once had coral eyes, too.

"I'm transmitting a vid of her from earlier tonight."

Liu's sick moan of pleasure made Dale feel a little sorry for Boston Maribu.

"She'll cost you double," Dale said. Hopefully he could make up for recent losses.

"Happily."

That made Dale feel a little *less* sorry.

"I'll have the money transferred into your account once she's in my possession."

Business as usual with Liu.

"See you soon."

As Dale ended his transmission, he thought of how Boston—Mari—had slipped through his fingers last year on Deleine. Her family had been right not to trust him. He wondered if he would have the same problems with the Armadan she was with tonight. If they had a relationship...no, she would have introduced him as her prime or at least as an amour. And surely any man who was involved with her wouldn't have stood by while Dale touched and caressed her the way he had. Although David Anlow had regarded him with a certain antagonism, but maybe that was simply the Armadan in him.

Not that Dale's interest went further than collecting his finder's fee on Mari. She was beautiful, yes, even with the exotic eye color, but he couldn't get past the idea that her genes were somehow polluted. Coincidentally, it was that very adulteration which made Liu willing to pay so high a price for her.

Apprehension crowded David's earlier happiness as they drew near the *Bard's* berth. Maybe he wasn't ready for the others to know about tonight. But how could he tell Mari that without insulting her? He pulled his arm away from her shoulders very delicately and took her small hands in his. "Mari, I think we should keep tonight our secret. I'm afraid the others—"

"Will ruin it?" she finished.

He was sure his surprise showed on his face. "So, you think so, too?" For some reason, now that she wanted to keep *him* a secret, he wanted nothing more than to walk on board and kiss her in full view of anyone who was around, which would probably be no one at this time of night.

"Sean already doesn't like you," she said.

A little twitch jumped into David's jaw thinking that she cared what Sean might think about tonight.

"And Kenon will never let up about it. Soli would make an official record of every time we looked at one another and say it was part of her archivist duties when we all know she can be nosy. And Geir, well, when he gets back, Geir would actually think it's about time, considering I told him how much I liked you. Besides, it's kind of exciting to sneak around."

"You confided in Geir?"

"Of course," she said, like it should have been obvious.

David wasn't sure how he felt about that—not that he didn't like the other Armadan, even if Geir chose a life outside the fleet. David just found he disliked how every guy around was more comfortable with Mari than he was. And Geir was halfway around the system right now.

David used his wrist reporter to lower the gangway to the *Bard* so that by the time they reached it, they could walk straight on board. As he suspected, no one was in sight. Soli and Kenon probably spent the night with their amours and Sean was no doubt brooding in his suite or drinking and dosing in some bar in the Latulip Underground.

Despite David and Mari being alone, or because they *were* alone, the apprehension slithered back under David's skin, putting him on high alert. He finally admitted that it had nothing to do with Mari or being caught with her. Feigning nonchalance, he scanned the shadowed areas around their berth and the next one over. It seemed fine.

Then the shadows moved.

Training took over, keeping his heartbeat steady, but readying his muscles and mind for action. "Mari, head inside the *Bard*."

The moving shadows morphed into six figures, all male. Judging by their slate grey workers' pants and stained shirts, David guessed they were Lower Caste laborers from the dock. Clothing was really the only way he could ever identify Lowers, because to him, they looked an awful lot like any other Socialite, except the homogenized contractors. But none of the old money Socialites from around here would believe that—they claimed they could tell just by looking at a person what their genetic background was. Of course, most Socialites only saw what they wanted to see.

It was then David noticed two contractors in the neighboring berth fifty meters away. Both males stood in the shadow of a dormant cargo off-loader that towered as high as a three story building so he couldn't quite see the men's faces, but he already knew who they were. And the clandestine nature of Killian and Ward's presence said they'd be no help with the ambush threatening Mari and him.

The dock workers wielded an array of tools from an electronic wrench as long as David's forearm to simple lengths of chain with massive links. And the men weren't afraid to brandish the makeshift weapons with ominous intent. Even a half-hearted swing of that electronic wrench could crack a man's skull in half. The same went for the bone-snapping links in those chains. But it was the hidden dangers that concerned David the most. Whatever they weren't advertising was undoubtedly nastier than something from a tool chest or construction site.

Mari curled a hand around his forearm.

He gently peeled her fingers away and whispered, "Mari, I need you to head for the ship and pull up the gangway as soon as you get inside."

"I'm not leav—"

"Please, Boston." He used her given name forcefully in hopes she understood the gravity of what he asked.

She scrutinized the men circling closer to them, then nodded in agreement. He noticed fear in her wide eyes, but she squared her shoulders and walked toward the *Bard*.

One of the men, dangling a chain and wearing a grease-stained hat, altered his course to intercept her.

"You take another step toward her and I will break both of your legs." David's sharp tone stopped the man's advance.

Mari paused before picking up her pace. Though David watched her climb the gangway, he kept each of the men in his periphery and was aware of their positions. He also noted the contractors finally moved a little closer, taking up prime spectator spots, eager for the fight they had been cheated out of earlier.

What kind of men let others do their fighting for them?

"This isn't your berth," a man with cropped blonde hair and prominent brows said. He was most likely the leader of this bunch, but maybe only because he looked a few decades older than the rest. David made careful note that the guy held nothing in his hands.

"Why do you care?" David rotated his left shoulder just enough to keep the hat-wearing worker and his shorter companions in sight. "I doubt the six of you could scrape together enough money for your own ship, so I'm sure you aren't the ones renting this space."

"Armadans are always so tight with money," the blonde man said. "They think they have more than everyone else in the system." The comment elicited a few mirthless laughs from his cohorts. Though he halted a good ten meters away, David didn't miss the bulge in the worker's waistline that confirmed he had a ranged weapon, like an illegal cender or pack of razor discs, which could inflict damage from a safe distance.

The last two men, more grizzled than their older counter parts, flanked David's right. That was a bad idea—they had put the *Bard*'s landing gear between them and an escape.

Lots of hard, protruding surfaces on that landing gear.

He was about to step toward them when a blur of movement came at him from the other direction. Hat guy swung the huge chain at David's head, the effort bobbling his balance. David ducked and twisted away before the metal links made contact. He kicked backward into the man's mid-section and knocked him off his feet.

The amber berth lights overhead glinted off metal back by the landing gear. The grizzled men rushed him with screams that belonged on a battlefield, not an urban dock. One brandished an electronic wrench, the other a sledgehammer. Snatching his first attacker up off the ground, David yanked the man in front of him just in time to take the full brunt of the wrench's blow. The splintering of a shoulder and clavicle was almost as loud as the man's screams. It stunned the guy who had swung the wrench long enough for David to shove his human shield into the man and propel them both into the landing gear. Their bodies hit hard and bounced down to the concrete.

The next man swung the sledgehammer at David's face. His opponent found out the hard way that Armadans didn't sacrifice much speed for their bulk. David caught the man's wrist mid-swing and jammed his fingers between the radius and ulna, pinching the sensitive tendons in a fleet technique used to disarm an opponent. The sledgehammer fell from the man's grip and clattered to the cement. He connected a lucky left hook to David's jaw. David forced the man's arm across his back until he heard the pop of a dislocated shoulder. The man screamed for release but David held onto his human shield.

The leader ordered the final man to move in, but he dropped his chains and went for more lethal weapons, a couple of small flat razor discs secreted in his waistband.

David swung his screaming shield into the discs' path. The multi-pointed blades thudded into the man's shoulder and jaw. He thrashed and pulled David's wrist reporter free as the man tried to pry his way out of the Armadan's iron grasp.

The edge of one disc snagged David, leaving a rough gash in his forearm. He tore the disc out and flung it at its owner, piercing the guy between the eyes and dropping him onto his knees then the dock.

"Shit." The blonde man's expletive drew David's attention to the cender he now gripped in a shaky hand.

He released an electric bolt before aiming. The shot sliced just above David's head.

"Don't shoot." The human shield's voice grated in pain. "You're going to hit me."

The gunner fired three more times into the sky behind them. David didn't flinch. He'd stared down cender fire, rifle fire and cannon fire. An aging dock worker with a cender ranked just above rude waiters on the list of things that scared him.

The gunner turned as Killian and Ward closed in on unhurried steps. "You said there wouldn't be any voyeurs." The man's voice trembled like his hands.

Ward fired his cender, a barely discernible hazy blue wake dropping the blonde dock worker to his knees. The man's weapon clattered to the concrete before he pitched forward onto his face.

From this distance David couldn't tell if Ward had dialed down his gun, rendering the man unconscious, or dialed it up for the kill. Still he smelled the ozone and burnt flesh all the way over here, and the hair on his arms was still standing from the surge of static electricity released into the night air.

David kept tight hold of the man drooping in his grasp, just in case Ward was still in the mood to shoot.

He aimed his cender at David, no doubt thinking it over.

Killian sauntered up to Ward and said, "I guess we should call in a med team and a prison transport. Why don't you take that guy off the retired captain's hands?"

Ward lowered his weapon, but it took him a good ten seconds before he finally holstered it, and only then because the errant voyeur the blonde man had seen floated closer to the scene.

The Media, ruining lives or spreading justice for entertainment. For once David was glad of society's obsession with transparency.

He pushed the dock worker in Ward's direction, making sure his hands would be full as David walked away.

He crunched over pieces of his wrist reporter that were now spewed across the concrete. At least they weren't bits of his skull. The dock workers, if they even worked here, could have caused him more bodily harm if they had had the foresight to catch him unawares. Or maybe they thought they had.

David looked back to watch Killian and Ward making arrests and calling in clean up and med crews as the voyeur recorded their every move. They'd come off as heroes, maybe get a bonus from the Embassy.

Killian called out to him. "We're going to need a statement from you later. Have a good evening."

A sick little thought entered David's head—if that stray voyeur hadn't happened by and witnessed at least part of the incident, Killian would be rounding David up, too, either for prison or the morgue. That had probably been the plan. Still might be.

"That was amazing," Mari said, peeking down from the top of the gangway. Her heart raced. "Smashing those guys' heads together. Throwing that one guy around like he was a doll." Then her praise turned to concern when David stepped into the light.

"Are you okay? You're bleeding."

"I'm fine." He pushed the manual control to raise the gangway.

"What happened to your reporter?" she asked.

"What happened to you locking yourself safely inside?"

She ignored his parental tone. "You may have needed help." She wiped blood from David's lip with her thumb and examined the nasty gash on his arm. "Come to the med suite. I'll patch this up for you."

"Out of curiosity…" As they walked, he put his uninjured arm around her in a protective gesture, still unsettled that she had been in harm's way. "What would you have done?"

"When?"

"If I had needed help?"

She searched his expression to see if he was making fun of her, but found his face full of earnestness.

"I would have called for someone to come… and help." She giggled a little as she said it, realizing how absurd it sounded out loud.

"Yeah, you could see those contractors were ready to jump right in," he said.

Mari could smell the tell-tale hint of antiseptic in the air before she activated the lights in the med suite. The soft blue of the floor and ceiling cut down on the glare.

"You didn't need them." She willed away the little tremble in her voice and her shoulders. Maybe David would think it was the cold instead of the incident just now,

46

but he was smarter than that.

He squeezed her closer and kissed the top of her head as they strolled past the green glass cabinets to the surgery.

"You'll have to sit down so I can reach you," she said.

David sat in one of the floating chairs, which didn't really float, only looked like it because they were attached to the wall by a support on their backs.

"Do you get into a lot of fights, like Sean?" she asked, searching the cabinet shelves for disinfectant and mender patches.

"I haven't been in a brawl since last year, and even then it wasn't my idea," David said. "Fighting is more my brother Ben's style."

"Which brother is Ben?" Mari asked.

"The one who bugs the shit out of me."

"Thought so." Mari placed all the medical items she needed on the counter beside David, but kept a pair of scissors in her hand. "Maybe I'll get to meet him one day. Like when you take me to see the forests at your family's estate." She hoped the reminder of this evening's earlier conversation about the beautiful mountains on Yurai would push away the ugliness of the recent violence.

"That would be nice." The way David responded sounded like he had already considered taking her.

She forced herself not to read too much into it and focused on sewing him up. "I'm going to have to cut off your sleeve."

"I think the shirt is pretty much a loss anyway."

"Well, you looked really nice in it," she said.

He gave her a little smile for the compliment.

"Did you have to do this for the miners often? Perform little surgeries?" he asked.

"Sometimes more than *little* ones." She didn't like to think about those days of tending to sick miners who barely had anything to live for anyway. They were often worse off than many of the Lowers here at the Hub, little more than indentured servants, paid by the ton. Just work, then home for a few days, then work again. Some even smuggled in their sons to get a bigger load out quicker—for what? A few extra items from the only store around, owned by the mining corporation? She shuddered, thinking that would have been her life...still could be.

"I was enamoured to a miner, or rather my family arranged the betrothal," she said, needing to share this information with David because her memories snapped at her in agitation. "I never accepted his proposal, and I'm not sure my family really forgave me for embarrassing them like that."

David remained silent so she kept talking.

"I couldn't do it. It felt so suffocating there, and not just because the air quality is so bad." Mari's voice became low.

David ran his palm up and down her back.

"My sisters are only a couple of years older than me," she said, "and already have several amours. I was a late start. I mean," she said quickly, hoping he didn't pick up on the real implication of her words, "I just didn't want to get married."

"Well, you are still a teenager," David said.

She shrugged out of his touch and put her fists on her hips, a mender in one hand and disinfectant solution in the other. "My age has nothing to do with it. I didn't want to marry *that* guy. Or any of the other ones I would have ended up with had I stayed on Deleine. They were nice, hard-working guys, but they were complacent, happy to spend the rest of their lives at jobs they hated."

"I'm proud of you for leaving, for following a different path than was laid out for you. That took courage."

"Thank you." The earnestness of his expression stirred such emotion in Mari. She had never had this kind of reaction to any man. Maybe because David was *so much* of a man. Strong, mature, commanding, smart, confident, good-looking— she could list his attributes the rest of the night, but he needed her to sew him up right now.

"I should put a couple of sutures in here before I put the menders on. The cut's deeper than I thought," she said. "Does this hurt? I can give you a stim patch." She swabbed the disinfectant over the area again, trying to be professional but unable to ignore the delight of touching David so intimately, of feeling like she was taking care of him. Most of her life someone had taken care of her. She was happy to be the responsible one for a change.

"It's fine," he said. "Just another battle scar."

"Oh, I'll make sure it doesn't scar." Then she asked, "Do you have real scars on your body?" Mari assumed the military had the most advanced healing and reconstructive technology in the system. Even her miners could walk away without many visible souvenirs of their wounds.

"I kept a few as reminders," David said.

"Really?" Mari suddenly felt a little too warm next to David in the med suite. "Can I...see them?"

"They're not all that exciting," he said, but showed her a halfmoon scar near the crook of his elbow. It was only a couple of centimeters long, but she was surprised she had never noticed it before.

"What did you do?" she asked.

"Ben did it. Took a chunk out of me with his teeth when he was four. I didn't tell anyone about it, just let it heal on its own, then kind of forgot about it after a while."

"You didn't want to get Ben in trouble?" Mari asked.

"No." David broke into one of his little smiles which always lit up his smoky eyes. "I didn't want to have to explain to our father how a four-year-old got the drop on his eleven-year-old brother. Now, I keep it to remind Ben what a pain in my ass he has always been."

"Is Ben your favorite brother?"

"Just the one who would never leave me alone."

Mari could tell David was joking. Family was so important to him, and despite the fact that she felt as though she had abandoned her own to chase her dreams through the stars, family was very important to her, too.

"Did Ben give you all your scars?" she asked.

"Not this one." David lifted his shirt to reveal a raised patch of flesh that left a dark zigzag starting only a few centimeters above his waistband and disappearing somewhere below it. Without thinking, Mari rubbed a thumb over the scar. A surge of arousal shot through her and settled right between her legs.

"What is this from?" Her words came out on a light breath as her pulse raced.

"A retractable electric whip, if you can believe it. They're actually illegal and extremely difficult to control, but the contractors we were engaging were rogues, so didn't care much about formal Embassy rules. If we hadn't been ambushed, and I would have insisted the team wear their armor, the whip would have never touched my skin. Instead it sizzled right through my fatigues and gave me a good zap and third degree burns. This one I kept to remember that Armadans are fitted with personal armor for a reason. So they can wear it."

"Uh huh," Mari said, only hearing half of what David had just said. She wanted more than anything to touch that scar again, and this time trace it all the way to its end. "How far down does it go?"

She felt her cheeks instantly flush, but curiosity had gotten the best of her.

"The scar? A couple more centimeters." He sounded amused.

"Oh." She busied herself applying the menders and acted as though she meant that as a clinical question. Then to push the point home, she made her voice as impersonal as possible and asked, "Would you like a stim patch for the pain?" Then remembered she had already asked him this question.

"I think I'll be fine without one."

He never flinched as the suture needle pierced his skin. She would have had to have a double dose of stims.

She made the sutures neat, but worked quickly.

"Okay, it's all finished," she said. "Keep the mender on for a day. The few stitches will dissolve on their own. I'll check the cut again later." She couldn't wait.

"Thanks for fixing me up." He took her hand and brought it to his lips.

Mari stood stock still.

They looked at each other for a moment. She broke the silence. "Do you want a drink?"

He seemed eager, then his expression changed and her heart fell even before the words came out of his mouth.

"I don't know. I have to write up this incident for the dockmaster and the local contractors' guild, though I'm sure my accusations will end up in a bureaucratic mound somewhere, never to be heard of again."

"That shouldn't take too long." She tried to nudge him without seeming desperate.

He rubbed her shoulder. "I want to know if you're okay after what happened tonight."

She flirted briefly with the idea of saying, 'No,' to see if that would make him change his mind about the drink, but was ashamed of herself for the thought.

"I'm fine." She fixed a smile on her face and decided to leave the night with her dignity intact. "I'm tired anyway. Thanks for a great evening, David."

She stood on her toes to kiss his cheek. He leaned down to meet her halfway and captured her kiss with his lips instead. Yearning spread through her entire body. It took all her reserve not to run her fingers through his thick hair and rub her body against him. She wanted him badly. Every nerve in her body tingled as she thought of where this kiss could lead.

Didn't he feel it, too? The heat? The pull of their bodies toward one another? The passion?

Her answer came when he broke away from her.

"Sleep well, Mari. I'll see you in the morning."

The bridge used to be a good spot to think.

David had always found solace in a nav chair, looking out upon the vastness of the system and its six planet-moons. But tonight, watching the stars from the confines of Tampa Quad instead of from the freedom of space, his mind wouldn't quiet. Maybe because he was on a modified pleasure cruiser instead of his warship. Or maybe the set up by the contractors still replayed in the back of his head. Or maybe he was just a little lonely tonight.

On the *Protector* there was no real night. Soldiers and technicians and diplomats, adjusting to multiple time zones on multiple planets, allowed for activity during the entire 25 hour cycle. But he wasn't captain of the *Protector* anymore, just a pilot on this little science craft.

David returned to the report he'd been compiling for the authorities. At first it worked to free his mind, the task of recording the events exactly as he remembered them from his encounter with the dock workers. His thoughts drifted, however, to the real reason he couldn't shake his restlessness. He wanted to be with Mari right now.

Was she still awake, thinking about what happened tonight? He could tell she was putting on a brave front, so he respected her need to show her courage and tried not to coddle her. Yet every instinct inside him screamed for him to go to her, to hold her and kiss her and whisper words of comfort—if not for her sake, then his.

She had invited him to continue their evening and he almost accepted. It was exactly what he wanted up until the moment she made it a reality, then he....

Then you ran away from her.

The thought pissed him off. What the hell was wrong with him? He'd led thousands

52

of men into battle, broken countless bones, endured hellacious conditions but was now afraid of one little blonde. Ridiculous.

Maybe he should call her room to be sure she was okay. Then he could tell by her voice if she was still up for company. And if she wasn't, he would be right back where he started, only more frustrated. He needed to stop this kind of thinking, tamp down his overactive hormones and concentrate on this damn report.

Yeah, right.

He was up from his chair before he could talk himself out of it. As he headed down the commonway, one by one he dismissed all the reasons why this wasn't a good idea…why he should find someone his own age…why he needed to distance himself emotionally from Mari…why he shouldn't be standing in front of her door at this hour.

He pressed the half-moon sensor of her door chime. When he could hear it sound loudly inside, he swore under his breath, feeling certain he had woken her. For what? He didn't have time to think of an excuse.

The door slid open.

"Hi." Mari's lazy smile and tiny green nightie made him want to dock her right there in the hallway.

"Hi." He felt a tad foolish, but more than a little excited. "I was working up the incident report and thought I should get your take on what happened. You do have that photographic memory."

Still can't admit why you're here, can you, Anlow?

"And to make sure you were really okay," he added.

Mari slid her arm through David's. "Nothing a drunken coffee won't fix. Do you want one?"

Say no.

He'd had more than enough alcohol tonight. Another drink and his judgment might be impaired. That was one of the reasons he didn't take the stims she offered from the med suite.

"What kind of bourbon do you have?" he asked.

"Koley's Reserve. What else?" She winked.

"You're kidding." He let his skepticism show. "Do you know how difficult that is to get? It's only made in the Koley Mountains, and in very small batches."

Even as an Armadan captain, he sometimes had to wait months for a bottle and he'd given his last one to the dockmaster as a bribe.

She just smiled that big smile of hers. "I wouldn't kid an Armadan about bourbon."

"Well, then how can I refuse a taste of home?" David took another quick survey of the strappy emerald-colored nightie draped over Mari's curves.

Once inside, the glowing vibrancy of her living quarters bombarded him.

"That's a lot of blue and green," he said.

"My favorite colors. It's a work in progress because you would not believe how much it costs to remodel one of these suites."

Now that she mentioned it, he could see traces of the original décor peeking from around billowing curtains and beneath thick area rugs and under an abundance of shiny pillows. For a soldier used to basic quarters, or even a man used to living alone in a sizable but modestly decorated lake house, the loud, plushy world Mari lived in was overwhelming.

It smelled great, though, thanks to all the flowering plants. In one corner of the foyer several large pots spilled over with blooms in varying shapes and sizes of white and turquoise petals while a blossoming vine twisted down from a wall-length stone planter inside the living room.

"You have a way with foliage. Or do you have some kind of secret grow lights?" he asked.

"I do monitor the lighting, but it's just the same lights you have in your suite."

Minus the aquamarine fringed lamp shades.

"I've been growing plants all my life," she said. "But this was the first time I ever tried in space. You'd think that with the artificial gravity and light it would be pretty much the same, but the plants know. So they take a little extra coaxing to flourish."

"Your coaxing is working quite well. They're amazing. And so many different varieties." He wanted to ask her specifics about a couple of plants on a stand nearby, but she had disappeared into the kitchen.

Being within her living space brought those waves of warmth back in a big way for David. Everything in this suite had been touched by her—bare toes on the cushy rugs, a brush of her hip as she passed by an end table, a subtle caress from her delicate hands as she cared for each bit of flora. David ran a finger down a hanging vine whose leaves looked like upside down hearts. They even had veins of red shooting through the waxy green exterior. He swore an electric tingle moved through his whole body from just this one little touch.

Get it together, soldier.

"I forgot I was out of coffee, but how about a drunken chai?" She handed him a mug.

He took a sip and almost couldn't swallow it, but forced the cloying liquid down his throat. "You like lots of sugar in your chai, don't you?" The sweetness nearly masked the aftertaste of alcohol.

"Like my mother always told me, everything is better with sugar." Mari sipped her drink and made a face.

So maybe she realized not *everything* was better with sugar, like expensive small batch malt.

"Sorry. Give me that." She grabbed his mug. "I really should have tasted it first. I'll sweeten it up a little."

David took both mugs from her and sat them on the counter. "I think I've had enough to drink."

"Really?" Her sly look burned right through him, impacting him below the belt. "Then I have something to show you." She took his hand and pulled him toward a room in the back. His mind immediately filled with images of bare skin sliding across bare skin, running his hands through her blonde hair, kissing parts of her he had only fantasized about, and....

She flicked on the lights with her wrist reporter. "How do you like my lab?"

David laughed, glad she hadn't been able to read his mind.

Mari's expression said she couldn't see what was so amusing.

He rubbed her back and tried to make the laugh seem like a natural response. "I can't believe how *great* this lab is."

Her eyes narrowed and he could tell she wasn't buying his feint.

"I'm sorry." He kissed the top of her head. "I wasn't expecting a lab back here." He looked around for the first time, taking in all the equipment and more plants. "Especially one so well-equipped. This must have cost a small fortune."

"It did, and until Dale offered me that job, I didn't have enough money to keep it. Look at this." She dragged David over to a mini-hydroponics unit enclosed like a greenhouse. Three white pipes hung down from a square unit in the ceiling. Small sprays of leafy plants stuck out of the pipe on all sides at ten centimeter intervals, each one holding a different type of greenery. Mari went about identifying them for him, but David's attention remained with her previous words.

For once, he didn't focus so much on Dale, but on the fact that Mari was struggling to keep her livelihood, her hard-fought independence. He couldn't imagine the pressure she had been feeling. Maybe Dale's appearance at dinner really was lucky for her. And David needed to control his jealousy, be happy for her. It's not like their relationship was serious. A couple of kisses and ambiguous innuendo didn't exactly show true progress, yet tonight he thought their connection deepened. Maybe it was the alcohol.

Mari laughed, startling him out of his thoughts. "I get it," she said.

He regarded her, wondering what he missed.

"You thought I was dragging you to bed," she said over her shoulder as she walked toward the door.

David smiled. "Maybe."

She waited for him in the doorway. "Well, the bedroom's this way." Grabbing his belt, she led him across the hall. He barely noticed the color surrounding him in this new space, just the flush of color that slid up Mari's bare back when he ran his fingers along her arms.

She dimmed the lights with a tap to her palm, activating her wrist reporter, then slid it off and threw it on the lime green rug. David snatched her off her feet and laid her on the bed, his gaze finding those beautiful coral eyes before his mouth covered hers.

Mari couldn't catch her breath because David stole it with each kiss. His hands were all over her—so were his mouth and his body. She hadn't expected him to be this aggressive, but she was thrilled by every second of it. Even the feel of his weight pinning her legs and hips to the bed.

His body was solid and muscled and the hardness of his arousal pressed through his pants. He covered her small frame until she felt cocooned by him and his wonderful scent. It was unlike anything she had ever felt before. Of course, anything dealing with coupling was new to her. Realizing that she would finally be with a man sent shivers down her spine.

That her first time would be with a man like David thrilled her.

Seeing him take on the six men at the dock stirred her desire even more than the memory of that beautiful kiss they'd shared. He easily handled situations that scared her silly. None of the men from her hometown commanded that kind of presence. Thinking about David dispatching their attackers made Mari kiss him with a fierceness she didn't know was inside her.

He responded by swirling his tongue into her mouth. Ever so slowly he slid his tongue over hers. She grabbed fistfuls of his thick, dark hair, becoming hyper-aware of certain parts of her body—her lips, her breasts, her....

"David," she gasped his name without completely breaking away from his skilled mouth. Her fingers fumbled for the buttons on his shirt. He worked from the bottom up until they met in the middle and she shoved the soft cotton away from his chest.

She had touched his chest in greeting dozens of times, but always the boundary of clothing kept her from his skin. The smooth feel of him now beneath her fingertips sent electric bolts through her body. His was the kind of body she and her sisters fantasized about. But here she was touching him, living the fantasy. She outlined his pectoral muscles, marveling at how his soft skin could cover such hard muscle. When she reached his nipples, she ran her thumbs over the erect little nubs, but shyness got the best of her, so she moved on, outlining the tops of his abs. She'd be happy just to touch him like this for the rest of the night.

David's hands were busy sliding the nightie from her shoulders, his mouth covering each centimeter of skin just after the fabric exposed it. He definitely knew what he was doing. Would he notice that she didn't? The thought suddenly bothered her. What if she disappointed him?

Determined that she wouldn't, she feigned a confidence that dwindled by the second. Reaching for his belt, she fumbled with the buckle. Her hands shook a little, but she managed to unfasten it and worked on the button of his pants next. That's when David's mouth found her breast, and she forgot all about his pants.

When his teeth teased at her nipple, she almost lost it. If he kept this up, he wouldn't need to go any further to bring her to climax. She groaned as his teeth were replaced with the tight grip of his lips.

Then she remembered the zigzag. With light fingers she moved down his belly until she brushed against the hard scar. She traced it, anxious to see where her hand would end up.

He kissed a line up her neck and whispered in her ear, "Still interested in that scar?"

"Uh huh," she mumbled, knowing full well his scar wasn't her biggest interest.

When she ran into the waistband of his shorts, she stopped, a little nervous to go any further, but her curiosity and desire won out. She slid her hand inside, keeping a finger along the scar until she found its end just above his thigh. But that was only a detour. She skated her fingertips across him in exploration until her hand brushed against his hardness.

"Maybe you should take your pants off," she said, gliding her fingers along his shaft.

"You first." He tugged at the nightie piled around her waist.

He kept kissing her neck as they wiggled out of their clothes, tossing garments to the floor and across the room.

Unrestricted by clothing, David's body was intimidating. Everything about him was so big. Granted, she was shorter than average and had a petite frame like her mother and half-sisters, but she had never felt smaller in her entire life than she did lying next to David.

"Such a sweet little body," he said. One of his big hands cupped her breast while the other one gently pushed her thigh aside to spread her legs. She hadn't realized she'd had them squeezed closed. He kept his hand there for a while, brushing the inside of her thigh with the back of his hand and his fingertips. She felt the wetness already trickling out of her as her folds started to open. And he hadn't even touched her there yet.

When he slid his hand between her legs, a little whimper of anticipation escaped her lips. With the first brush of his fingers against her clit, the whimper became a moan. Sensation shot through her body as two of his big fingers made delicate circles, teasing her open further. As he increased the pressure and speed of his massage, she closed her eyes with the delight of it.

She ran her hands down his back to the top of his backside where she squeezed his toned flesh as her body built to climax. How many times had she wanted to touch him, to have him touch her just like this? Part of her couldn't believe it was actually happening. As if to convince her of reality, her orgasm hit, rocking her body until she was squeezing David's hand between her legs as each wave swelled and crashed.

She was still writhing with pleasure when he withdrew his hand and shifted position. But when she felt his hardness press at her opening, she froze. Almost reflexively, she pulled her knee up to put distance between their bodies.

"Everything okay?" he asked.

"Sorry. Some of this is just a little new for me." She slid her knee from between them, but couldn't force the stiffness from her body. Or the sudden bout of shivers.

"What are you saying, Mari?" David sounded tentative, as though he already knew the answer.

"I haven't…exactly done this before, but I want to," she said quickly, tightening her grip on his neck to emphasize her enthusiasm. "Please don't be mad. You could show me what to do." Her emotions were getting the better of her as disappointment and embarrassment flooded through her. That's when the tears blurred her vision. She felt foolish admitting her inexperience to a man like David. Well, maybe to any man, but especially David.

"Mari, honey." David brushed away the tears on her cheek with his thumb. "I'm not angry with you." He kissed her forehead then both of her closed eyes. "I'm just surprised." He stroked her hair and spoke in a soothing tone. "It means we should take this a little slower."

"I'm tired of taking it slow, David. You were the first guy I wanted to do this with. And now I've ruined it."

"You haven't ruined anything." He kissed her slowly and with such tenderness she knew he meant what he said. "Slow can be fun," he murmured.

His mouth trailed down her neck. She'd always seen couples do this on the Media and sometimes in public spaces at Shiraz and outside the high end shops of Latulip. It had looked blissful to her. When David went from kissing to gently sucking at the sensitive skin below her ear, she decided bliss couldn't come close to describing the sensation.

"Slow is definitely fun," she whispered.

Last night was unexpected.

David had never been someone's first, had never wanted the responsibility. After coupling with Mari, he couldn't imagine the experience being any more satisfying… and emotional. Not just for her. Sharing her first coupling made him regard her with awe and respect, and whether he wanted to admit it or not, it made him want to make their new relationship a little more permanent. Suddenly he didn't care if his hormones were telling him to settle down—so was his heart. It was his head that kept getting in the way. If his decision to retire early was what brought that settling down idea front and center, it meant he shouldn't even be considering it until he'd had enough time away from the fleet to clear his head.

His contentment upon waking faded a little as he worried that what he felt for Mari was simply an emotional fallacy. Not that he believed his feelings for Mari were false, he just didn't trust them to make any life decisions for him after Lyra. The fact that he was already contemplating taking his prime based on how he felt in the after-glow of a night of coiting with a teenager practically screamed for him to put as much distance between Mari and himself as humanly possible.

She was already acting as though their tryst had sealed some sort of deal. When she spoke of it, he hadn't discouraged her, though. Instead, he let her indulge them both with her fantasies. Even now, with his rational mind reprimanding him, David still wondered how it might feel to wake up next to her each morning, her tousled blonde locks hiding her face and her thin arm thrown possessively over his bulky chest. Just like now.

He slept over very few nights with women, but he sure as hell wasn't going to leave Mari alone after her first time. At least that's the lie he told himself when he agreed to stay last night. Was that also the reason he kept her curled next to him, never taking a hand off her the entire time?

She gave him a new purpose. Mari was the first person he had met who didn't worry about his rank, about his influential family, about what he could do for her—well, she did like what he could do for her. He smiled because the feeling of being wanted by a woman just because he was a man was new to him, despite, or maybe because of, the hundreds of trysts he'd had over his years in the fleet. His own family joked about him being somewhat of a whore, but what they didn't realize was that, in the beginning at least, he was just looking for a companion.

After too many disappointments at a young age, he gave up on the more meaningful part of sex and pursued just the physical side.

Until Lyra. Lovely Lyra. He'd never called her that to her face because she would have thought the endearment too sentimental.

He admitted he steered their relationship in a direction she hadn't wanted—she was a career military woman, ten years younger than him. A family life didn't register in her plans any time soon. Sometimes, in reflective moments like this, David feared he pushed her into mutiny. She made their stifling relationship part of her warped reasoning for trying to take over his ship. Maybe that's why the fleet washed away the incident…and promoted her. Better than dealing with a possible harassment suit, though he'd never overstepped his boundaries. It wasn't in him to break the rules, even for Lyra. He'd probably never know the truth of what happened with her upward mobility within fleet ranks. That was fine with him. In fact, David hoped he'd never see Lyra again.

Mari lifted her head and blinked sleepy eyes through the hair tumbling over her face. "Good. You're still here," she said.

Her sweet voice and genuine delight in seeing him instantly banished cold thoughts of Lyra. Even at nineteen, Mari was ten times the woman Lyra would ever be.

He pressed his lips against her tousled hair. "I don't think I could have gone anywhere if I wanted to." He looked pointedly at her arm and leg flopped over him.

She smiled and rolled off him, pulling the sheet with her. Her shyness transferred to David and he kicked his feet over the other side of the bed and grabbed his shorts and pants.

"You don't have to go," she said as she made her way into the bathroom.

"I need to check with the dockmaster this morning, let him know we'll be staying a little longer."

Mari poked her head out of the bathroom and said, "That's right. I forgot about that meeting with Dale today."

Wish you would forget about Dale permanently.

David had to remind himself that her enthusiasm was for the job, not for the man, but that didn't make him any less annoyed. After last night David's protective instinct sped into high gear concerning Mari. He had never felt this need to be so shielding of any other women he'd been intimate with. He explained it away because of her age and her inexperience, because she was a Socialite not a competent battle maiden, but his instinct came from a place inside him that housed much deeper feelings, a place he wasn't ready to visit just yet.

She bounded around the corner, her red-tipped blonde hair pulled into a high ponytail, a short, flower print robe in place of the sheet. As she chattered about plans for that day, he imagined having many mornings like this with her and it made him happy.

Except not in this room.

Seeing Mari's bedroom in full light, with blues and greens in wild prints and patterns covering every available square centimeter, even creeping onto the ceiling, would have been somewhat comical if it weren't almost terrifying. The fuzzy throw pillows alone would have sent a lesser man running for the door.

"Maybe we could get lunch after I see Dale?" she suggested. "You could either come with me to Wright's Landing or we could meet in the Hub."

Stay out of her business.

"I can go with you to see Dale," he said.

"Great." She bounced up to his chest and gave him a peck on the lips. "Meet you in half an hour under the trees?"

She confused him again until he realized she meant the giant glass trees in the *Bard*'s foyer. The azure arcs of light flowing inside them still mesmerized him from time to time, just like watching Mari did.

"Under the trees," he said.

David couldn't believe he had to ask Sean for another reporter. The mech tech would never let him hear the end of it. At least it would be a good excuse to ask for an interface with the *Bard* again. He pressed the entry sensor and heard a tell-tale chime on the other side before the door slid open.

Sean stood fiddling with some piece of circuitry in the middle of his sitting room, which was still decorated in the gaudy style of an old pleasure cruiser—one that hadn't been visited by housekeeping in the last twenty years. Alcohol bottles and empty droppers added to the narcotic den ambiance and confirmed David's suspicions that Sean Cryer was a doser and an alcoholic.

"I lost my reporter," David said.

Sean didn't look up from the mass of wires and parts splayed across his coffee table. "When did you lose it? I need to lock out all the codes so someone can't access the ship."

"No worries there. It's completely obliterated."

"How did you manage that? I thought you were used to running an entire war ship."

"It's a long story, but since you bring up the war ship thing, can you finally update my cerebro implant so I can interface with the *Bard* directly?" David asked.

"Is that still illegal for civilian pilots?" Sean asked.

They both knew it was, but Sean didn't seem like the type of guy who cared much about legalities. David thought after a couple of weeks the younger man would start to trust him. Sean's substance abuse made him paranoid. Maybe he thought David was testing him. Whatever Sean's problem, David didn't have time to argue with him today.

"Then just give me another reporter," David said. "*They're* still legal, aren't they?"

"Last time I checked." Sean disappeared into a back bedroom. When he emerged, he tossed a thin silver bracelet at David.

He snatched it up before it hit the tile floor. "Thanks. You're all kinds of helpful."

"Works best if you use this finger." Sean held up his middle finger in a crude good-bye.

"You're an ass. By the way, we're staying an extra day here at the Hub."

That got Sean's attention. "What the hell for? So you can make a point?"

"It's for Mari. She's meeting with a client."

Sean didn't say anything more, but his expression said he wasn't happy. That would have normally made David smile, but he was too wrapped up in thoughts about Mari's meeting.

He strapped the reporter on his wrist. "You ever hear Mari talk about a former client named Dale Zapona?"

"The name sounds familiar. Why?" Sean asked.

"I met him last night. Something's off about him, but he seems to be interested in Mari doing a job for him, bringing his latest ship up to greenshift code," David said, agitation working into his jaw as he remembered Dale's sleazy advances toward Mari.

Either David's thoughts showed on his face or Sean came to the same conclusion. "You think he wants to dock her."

"Seemed that way when he was talking to her. But I don't think Mari got the same impression from him."

"She probably didn't. Mari's naiveté is going to get her into trouble one of these days. The wrong guy could take advantage of her trusting nature." Sean's tone gave David the impression that Sean was hinting at someone a little closer to Mari.

Does he know about last night? Because Sean's attitude could be construed as jealousy. The idea that Sean might be interested in Mari struck David hard and it came out in his tone.

"You don't know her as well as you think you do."

Sean did something then that David had never seen the mech tech do in the month he'd known him—he smiled. Just a little upturn to the corner of his mouth, but it was enough to nearly drive David into a rage. He shoved into the commonway before he could use his clenched fists to smash that smile right off Sean's face.

Sean tapped his palm to activate his implanted wrist reporter, making the already loud music raise to ear-shattering heights within the confines of his bedroom. The pounding beats and anti-Embassy lyrics spat out on angry tongues soothed him...or maybe it was the restor patch he'd just jabbed into his hip. Whether through narcotic bliss or aural disorientation, he relaxed against the bed's bare mattress and took a deep breath. He snagged a case from the empty night table and popped the metal clasp. A tinny smell accosted him. Inside, swimming in clear conductor fluid, were what looked like two silver, opaque contact lenses. They were v-mitters and they allowed his consciousness to merge easily with an electro-magnetic stream opening directly to the V-side.

Preparing to enter the universe of the virtual world made him feel like going home. More so, considering he held power as a fragger node inside the V-side while at his childhood home on Tampa Quad there was only the helplessness of grief that touched every part of him. Somehow his mother had overcome the loss of both her prime amour and eldest son, but Sean just shoved their deaths further inside himself. Once there the memories of the two men in his life warped over the past decade and a half—he now associated them more with pain and abandonment than anything else. It might not be a fair association, but in his mind it rang true.

When David first came aboard the *Bard*, feelings which Sean hadn't felt in years suddenly hounded him, not all of them unpleasant, like maybe this was how Sean's father had been when he was alive, before combat and duty took him. Or how Sean's brother Jameson might have turned out. Jameson was always bigger, had the stronger bearing, even as a teenager, but it turned out Jameson didn't have any guts—otherwise he wouldn't have killed himself at sixteen and left behind a heart-broken mother and little brother.

Sean had turned to a new family, the fraggers. Their anti-caste, anti-government sentiments filled his emptiness and made him strong against his grief, if not a bit hardened toward life. A softness remained in his heart for his mother, for most women really. That's why he was so protective of Mari. She might annoy him with her constant chatter and immature notions, but she was a kind, beautiful person with a great mind. He'd entertained certain thoughts about her when she first arrived on the *Bard*, then realized how old she was and decided they'd be better as friends.

Now she was friends with David.

The idea bothered him. He wouldn't exactly call it jealousy—he just didn't like having to worry about her. Of course there probably wouldn't be anything to worry about as far as David Anlow was concerned. The man was by the book and unruffled in every aspect of his life. The military may have drummed discipline into him, but it also bound him to rules and societal expectations. For Sean, too much of life had to be lived outside the rules, outside the law, in fact. Would David ever break the law, even for reasons beyond the law itself? Sean thought not, and that's why he had a problem with the ex-fleet captain.

His thoughts of David drifted away with the cool sensation spreading behind Sean's eyes into his brain. Within a few seconds the pressure changed inside his head, announcing the arrival of his avatar Zak into the floating V-side lobby. An endless ocean of gentle purple waves met a silvery sky in this alternate reality which was just a step beyond dreaming. His av Zak stood alone on a meter square platform, undulating with the soft roll of the lobby's sea while Sean's body remained safe aboard the *Bard*. Should anyone come into his bedroom, it would simply look as though he were in a deep sleep.

But his senses were active, all except his ability to smell—once the architects found a way to make scent active within the V-side the experience would truly become immersive. His synapses fired, processing his environment as though Sean were physically there, not just represented by Zak. He could even feel and react to the moving balance of the slate-colored raft as the sea lapped beneath it.

Invites to multiple worlds within the V-side awaited him in the form of small, blue globes the size of Sean's fist. The lighter the shade of blue, the more important the invite. Sean still ignored them all, even one powdery blue one from a fragger boss.

He hadn't been officially summoned so whatever it was could wait until he found out about Mari's new business associate.

Sean didn't even plan to enter a V-side world right now, just wait in the lobby for Bullseye, one of his fragger contingency whom he trusted with the delicate nature of information gathering.

A second pop preceded the appearance of a second raft. A young man with green spiky hair waved. "Hey, Zak! Found what you wanted."

Bullseye was always eager to please. What the man, if indeed he even was male, did in real life, Sean couldn't say. For security reasons, no one except the bosses knew any other fragger's identity. That's why Sean was Zak, a generic-looking blonde guy whose features only vaguely resembled his own and whose build was much smaller than Sean's actual half-Armadan frame.

"Thanks, Bullseye. What's the deal with Dale Zapona?"

"He's squeaky clean."

"In other words, he's hiding something," Sean said in Zak's voice, a tad more tenor than the real thing.

"You better believe it. Take a look."

A tingle sparked to life in the back of Sean's mind as he received the data from Bullseye. He processed the official Embassy file and found markers where sections had been deleted at the source. The Embassy tech who had performed the erasure did a better job than most Sean had run across, but still left a dusting of code like a trail of sand leading to each instance of removal.

"That Dale guy has friends in high places," Bullseye said.

"Looks that way. I appreciate your help with this, and your discretion."

"No problem." Bullseye hesitated, then said almost sheepishly, "I'm heading to a slasher session with some of the other guys. You want to join us? We could use you to balance out the teams."

"Not this time."

Bullseye's expression read disappointment, though Sean never took any facial or body cues as sincere in the V-side—it was too easy to program certain responses and call them up as desired. However, since Sean's contingency was always trying to get him to enter a gaming world with them, Bullseye's reaction was probably honest. Sean just didn't like to get too close to anyone in here. Or anyone out there, he decided as he unplugged to rejoin the real world.

"Thank you for coming with me," Mari said to David. "I'm a little nervous. How's my outfit? Is it too stuffy?" She had tried to dress practically. This morning the little grey skirt, which rode a bit high on her thighs, and the white sleeveless blouse which plunged a bit low at her neck, seemed like a good idea. Of course, she didn't really own anything practical, so this was the least ostentatious outfit she could come up with.

"Definitely not too stuffy," David murmured.

Her head snapped around. "Should I have tried to look more scientific?" She had no idea how she would do that.

David's warm hand cupped her bare knee and gave it a little squeeze as the Wrights Landing transport curved past another private gate leading to a palatial stretch of grounds. She'd been so pre-occupied she'd missed the gardenia bloom on the way here.

"You look nice," he said. "The important thing is you know more about hydroponics systems than anyone I've ever met. You're ready to take the greenshift head on."

"How many other botanists have you met?" she joked, happy that David had taken an interest in her career. Not even her family had. Or maybe they simply couldn't understand her need to be more than a mother, not that she wasn't looking forward to that role, especially now that she had become so close to David. She imagined more than a few times since their coupling session about conceiving with him. She'd keep those thoughts to herself, however. After all, last night was only her first time. If she convinced Dale to give her this contract, she and David could have many nights together.

And if Dale decided not to hire her…she'd probably have to go back to Deleine. A sickness roiled in her stomach at the possibility.

"Here we are," David said.

Anxiety flooded through Mari as the transport waited at the elaborate wrought iron gate marking the entrance to Dale's estate. The metal relief of a massive tree with exposed roots and gnarled limbs devoid of leaves loomed in front of them.

"That is the ugliest, scariest tree I've ever seen," Mari said.

David smiled as he helped her out of the transport. He had such a nice, subtle smile. She kept hold of his hand, maybe clenching it a bit too tightly. If she returned home would he come to visit her? Maybe at first, but it would only be for a few sporadic weeks throughout the year until maybe he couldn't come at all or wouldn't want to. Suddenly the pressure of winning Dale over veiled her in sadness.

David must have caught her mood.

"Dale isn't the only client in the system, you know. If this doesn't work out, there are other options. Just a matter of finding them."

She appreciated David's encouragement, but she knew the truth—it was this job or nothing.

A tall man with cropped blonde hair met them inside the gate. The elegant cut of his grey suit and light blue button-down shirt couldn't disguise the mass of muscles beneath.

"Is he an Armadan?" Mari asked.

"Looks like it." David's tone took on a slight derision. "Merc-ing himself out as a bodyguard apparently. I guess no rogue contractors were available."

The blonde Armadan looked at David like he was unwelcome. Maybe Mari should have mentioned to Dale specifically that David would be coming with her, but she hadn't thought it necessary.

She took the initiative, hoping her confidence and use of formal titles would persuade the Armadan that this had been the plan all along. "Hello, I'm Scientist Boston Maribu and this is Navigational Leader David Anlow. Chairman Zapona is expecting us."

"The chairman is expecting *you*, Scientist Maribu," the bodyguard said. "I'm not sure he understood you would be bringing a guest."

She chewed on her lip.

David spoke up. "Dale's well aware I would be accompanying her after our meeting at Shiraz last night. Maybe you should ask him."

She didn't miss the fact that David used Dale's first name, maybe that familiarity would work in place of her formality.

"I already contacted Chairman Zapona when you arrived," the Armadan guard said. "Since you're here, he's happy to welcome you both into his home."

Mari wasn't convinced of that by the man's inflection.

"My name is Carlos. Please follow me."

This wasn't the start she had been hoping for today. She dropped David's hand and donned a serious expression, hoping her professionalism would show through to Dale.

"Chairman Zapona thought you would enjoy meeting in his conservatory," Carlos said. "It's through the garden."

Another iron gate, matching the one at the entry, fit snugly into a towering stone wall which went along the property as far as Mari could see.

"That must be his house behind there." Mari kept her voice quiet so only David could hear her as she gestured with her chin at the steepled roofs peeking from behind the wall and the large palm trees somewhere on the other side.

"Looks like," David said in a distracted voice as he scanned the gardens in front of them.

He considered his surroundings with such focus, even studying the erratic flight of a butterfly as though it carried a secret upon its wings. His behavior only served to unnerve her more.

Mari teetered on her heels as they crunched through the pea gravel strewn along the main track. David offered her an elbow to steady herself as they walked. She appreciated that Dale wanted to go natural, but not at the expense of her ankles. And this was probably ruining her shoes.

Enticing pathways lined with vibrantly colorful flowerbeds wove through the walled garden. In all, it must have covered four hectares. Footpaths narrowed off to secret spots with benches waiting under trees and burbling fountains. Along both sides of the winding main conduit stretched well-ordered beds in blooms themed by fragrance and color.

"It smells so good here," she said.

"Like your suite," David said. "And, it's just as colorful." His tone was playfully mocking.

At the path's terminus, a glass and steel building greeted them. The interior appeared to be stuffed with as much foliage and flora as the garden surrounding it. The humidity hit them as soon as Carlos opened the door.

"He had to have this meeting in a sauna, didn't he?" Beads of perspiration dotted David's hairline.

Mari actually felt quite comfortable, but David had an extra hundred kilograms of muscle to carry around.

She paused inside the double glass doors. "You don't have to come in if you don't want to."

He waved her off. "I'm fine, just occasionally prone to complaining."

"This way," Carlos said with a touch of impatience in his voice.

She didn't miss the antagonizing looks he and David exchanged.

The conservatory sheltered rare palms and tropical vines and had an entire wing devoted to orchids. Dale sat at a table surrounded by these botanical gems, which showed off their brilliance in the glass-walled room. A nest of bedding plants were tucked in another wing, ready to replace any of the exterior florae which might die off and spoil the perfection of the design. This elegant space with its exotic greenery should have brought a sense of peace to Mari, but as she faced Dale, her stomach tightened. It was time to prove her worth.

Dale stood to greet them, wearing a crisp, blue tunic and casual pants. Though quite a few centimeters taller than Mari, Dale looked diminutive next to the Armadan males. What he missed in height and bulk, he made up for in a brilliant, white smile.

"So glad we can have this meeting, dear."

She noticed he completely ignored David, as though he were nothing more than a hired bodyguard like Carlos.

"This is really just a formality," Dale continued. "The job is yours if you want it."

"Just like that?" David asked

Mari shot him a look, but he stared at Dale.

"I have your curriculum vitae from the last time I wanted to hire you and I would assume you've only added to your wonderful resume since then."

The excitement Mari felt at being offered the contract waivered ever so slightly upon mention of her *wonderful* resume. It had been less than stellar back on Deleine— Dale had even commented on that at the time. And except for a couple of landscaping jobs for hire when she first came to the *Bard*, her skills list hadn't grown much. Even with her mine experience, she couldn't boast any work that had to do with designing a hydroponics system for a freighter.

She pushed the needling doubt away to concentrate on what Dale was saying now.

"We can leave tomorrow. I'll just have Carlos provide you with the proper documents—"

"Leave?" Mari asked.

"Yes, the *Thrall 7* will depart for its run back to Deleine tomorrow, hopefully with our new botanist on board," Dale said.

"I'll be working on the design on-site, in-transit?"

"Of course, dear. The design process alone takes a few weeks, no? Add another month for installation. That is much too long for the *Thrall* to be off route."

"I wouldn't think I'd have to be on-site to oversee the installation," Mari said.

"I would insist upon it, dear. Don't you want to make sure the mech techs don't corrupt your beautiful design? There will be several cargo stops to and from Deleine, so consider it a way to see more of the system on your off-time."

"Aboard a freighter? That sounds like fun," David said.

"I'm sorry," Dale said. "What's he doing here?"

"Moral support," David said.

Mari gave David a pleading look. "Maybe you could give us a minute?" she asked.

David's visage remained unreadable. When he finally pulled his attention away from Dale to look at her, she wondered if he would refuse to leave, but he surprised her with a small kiss. "I'll be outside, in the shade, if you need me."

"Thank you," she said.

Maybe if David weren't standing right beside her she could think more clearly about Dale's offer. It wasn't exactly what she had anticipated, but six weeks away from David was better than losing her suite on the *Bard* and maybe never seeing him again.

"Your pilot's quite friendly." Dale broke into her thoughts. "Or maybe he's just marking his territory?"

He waited for Mari to respond, but she remained uncharacteristically quiet. She was afraid anything she said might make Dale reconsider. Maybe it wouldn't be so bad if he did. If she walked away from this job, others would be out there. Isn't that what David had insisted when they first arrived?

"He's not your amour, is he?"

"No," Mari said quickly. "We're…friends and we share a lot of our time together on the *Bard*." She could feel the heat rising into her cheeks, giving her away. "It's a small ship."

Dale walked closer. *"Very* intimate accommodations, I imagine."

She studied the light blue polish on her fingernails to avoid looking at Dale, but still caught the leer peeking from the side of his mouth.

"The *Thrall* isn't like your refurbished pleasure cruiser, but you'll see that it can still be surprisingly intimate."

The remark brought that needling caution back into Mari's mind. What if Dale wanted more than a hydroponics bay from her?

"May I have a little time to think about this?" Mari asked. "I know you're scheduled to leave tomorrow, so I would let you know by morning. Please, don't think I'm ungrateful. I just have to put some things in order."

"Not a problem, dear." He leaned in to say, "A word of advice, though. Armadans are a pushy lot. If you don't show your nav leader that you won't be ordered about like a crewman, he'll expect your obedience to his every whim forever after. Very similar to the situation you left at home, as I recall."

Mari didn't disagree. In fact, she said nothing as she left.

Dale watched Mari depart through the glass door. "The Armadan will be a problem. He already has influence over her. I could see it in their body language. He'll convince her not to take my offer so that he doesn't lose her."

"What do you want to do about it?" Carlos asked.

"Not give her a chance to say no. The other women didn't have that luxury. Why should this one?"

"I don't think a simple abduction would be so *simple* with the pilot in the picture. He's an ex-fleet captain and he didn't get to that position without a few fights along the way."

"You don't think you can handle him?" Dale smirked.

Carlos's fair skin flushed a light pink. "I can deal with him, but storming their ship and prying the blonde out of his arms would be a huge mistake."

"We have the best law team money can buy. I've never had a conviction because I pay our Sovereign a hefty insurance fee, plus he's family. He'd never let a cousin, no matter how distant, be caught up in any *trouble.*"

"It's not just the legal issues I'm concerned about. This would be personal to the Armadan."

"Who cares? Once we have her, he can't do anything about it."

Carlos shook his head in frustration. His tone was clipped when he spoke, as though he were holding back. "With respect, chairman, you have never served in the fleet. It is its own world, with its own rules and codes of conduct. Its own *justice*. You snatch that woman from him outright, you better kill him because he won't stop until he finds you. And, if you kill *him*, he has brothers and cousins, and men and women he served with who will come kicking your door down just to see you bleed."

Dale snickered, shattering the heaviness of Carlos's words so the man couldn't see how much they impacted him. "Every Armadan I've ever met enjoys making idle threats and grandiose promises of retribution. Let's face it, the military is for show. I haven't heard of one combat-related engagement from the mighty fleet in decades. Nobody has." He stabbed a finger in the larger man's face. "Because you all bulk up, flex your inflated muscles, and stand around playing with each other until your tour is finished. The Sovereign keeps you around because the appearance of a strong military makes him look stronger."

Carlos stepped forward. "You never hear about any fleet involvement because *your Sovereign* wants it that way. I may have gotten tired of being a trooper, but I still know what goes on in the Armada."

Though Dale held his ground for as long as he could, he finally stepped back, making for his seat once again as though he were dismissing Carlos. A small shiver ran up his back even in the humidity as he avoided looking into the Armadan's dark eyes. He may have pushed too far, but Carlos wouldn't be foolish enough to cut the throat of his money man.

"I'm open to ideas, then. How do we make this business with the woman easier? Something that won't implicate either of us?" Dale asked.

"Don't let Dale strong-arm you into taking this job," David said. "You don't need him." The argument which had started shortly after lunch came to a head as Mari and David disembarked from the ferry.

All the pushy passengers, most of them taller than her and not all of them fresh-smelling, made her feel claustrophobic, adding to her agitation.

"I *do* need him," she said between clenched teeth when they broke free of the largest part of the crowd.

"He just wants you to think that."

"Why would he want that?" Could David not understand the direness of her predicament?

"Because what he's *really* after has nothing to do with botany. I can't believe you don't see this yourself." David's exasperated tone and raised voice made her feel like a child.

"How would you know, David? Did he tell you he wanted to dock me or did you just assume that's the only reason he'd hire me?"

It didn't matter that she had been thinking the same thing since the meeting. Hearing David reveal his thoughts out loud hurt her because she thought he had been the only one to believe she was capable.

"Mari—"

"Like I would dock him anyway. Did you ever consider that? I already have a father, David. I don't need another one." She hadn't meant for the comment to sting, but Dale's words about obedience crowded her thoughts.

"Is that how you think of me?" David's tone changed, the anger slipping away. "I didn't realize the age difference bothered you."

"It's not your age. I just thought you understood how important this was to me." The pedestrians sharing the boardwalk with them stared as Mari's voice rose with emotion.

David put a hand on her arm. "Mari, let's talk about this back on the ship."

She wouldn't look at him and didn't stop walking, forcing him to keep moving with her. As they made their way back along the boardwalk to the *Bard* she dismissed thoughts of their first kiss. The light of late afternoon helped—it didn't have the same ambiance as the glittery evening.

"If I don't take this job," she said, "I'll have to go home. Back to Deleine."

"That seems a little drastic."

She snapped her head around. "I'm out of money, David. My family was right. They said I'd return within a year. I barely made it eight months. I can hear the I-told-you-so speeches already."

The thought of her parents and siblings, everyone in her huge family circle, being right about her failure made her resolute—she'd do whatever it took to stay off Deleine. If it meant six weeks away from the *Bard* and David, she'd have to suck it up and go. If he didn't want her when she got back, she'd deal with that possibility when it came. Thinking that he actually might *not* want her made her feel a little betrayed.

Wanting to put some emotional distance between them, she pulled ahead of him inside the foyer.

"Mari, I think we should talk about this," David called to her.

"Not right now, okay?" She wanted to be alone because she didn't want to cry in front of him and could feel the pressure of angry, frustrated tears building behind her eyes.

"So that's it? You're just going to walk away from me instead of discussing this–"

She spun around on the bottom step of the grand foyer. "You want me to talk? Then listen. Dale is my last chance. Sean has already been paying the lease on my suite for the past two months, and I'm still a month in arrears. It's not fair to keep asking him for money, even though he tells me I don't have to pay him back. Designing Dale's system for the next six weeks is the only way I don't have to pack everything and go home next month. If Dale still wants me in the morning, I'm taking his offer. Though he might get tired of waiting for me by then, especially after today."

It stung her pride to admit her short comings and how much she had been relying on others. So when David didn't respond right away, her anger rose and she started up the stairs.

David zipped up to join her. "Mari."

"I'm really tired, David, and I need to talk to my family about this." She spoke as she continued climbing the staircase.

"That's a good idea." He rushed to get in front of her and block her progress. "But can you and I talk first? I'm just now hearing about some of this and haven't had time to process it all. I know you said your finances were running low, but I didn't realize Sean was lending you money. We can work something out to make sure you don't have to leave. I don't want to see that happen any more than you do."

Her heart bumped a little harder with his words.

"Talk with me, just for a minute." He rubbed her shoulder.

She was about to agree when she heard footsteps on the stairs behind her. David pulled his hand away like she was toxic. It was the final blow to her already bruised ego. She looked over her shoulder to confirm that the approaching trudge of boots was indeed Sean. He staggered a little and had to grasp the handrail opposite them.

When David stepped away from her, she felt a pang of humiliation, then scorn. After the amazing night they'd spent together, she expected…what did she expect from David? Some kind of acknowledgment of their relationship. Even if he had no emotional attachment to her after they docked, that didn't mean he should act like they were barely friends anymore when someone came by.

Mari's frustration got the best of her. She met Sean halfway up the stairs, sliding under his shoulder and wrapping an arm around his waist. He stopped in his tracks.

"You look like you need help getting to bed," she said.

He looked at her like she had three heads. David would think it was just the alcohol, but Mari knew Sean was baffled by her behavior.

David's jaw tightened and he gave Mari one last look before shaking his head in what she assumed was disgust and walked down the stairs. Sadness washed over her. She hated to admit that a small part of her hoped David would get jealous enough to rip her out of Sean's less-than-enthusiastic embrace. It would have at least been a public acknowledgment that David cared for her.

"That was a bad move," Sean said. "You're playing a risky game with a guy like David."

"What do you mean?" Mari asked, pretending she wasn't just thinking the same thing.

"You know exactly what I mean. *Helping me to bed?* This kind of behavior will backfire, especially using me to try and make him jealous. He can't stand me."

"I thought you couldn't stand him," Mari said.

"We have a mutual antipathy for one another."

"You're quite eloquent when you're drunk."

As if in direct opposition to her compliment, he grunted and guided her up the stairs with light hands on her shoulders.

It's not all her fault.

David had been pacing the black floor of the bridge since that ugliness on the stairs a couple of hours ago. He was as much to blame for it as Mari was. Maybe more so. He finally convinced her to open up, then pulled away, leaving her feeling vulnerable and unwanted. It had given her the wrong impression.

No, it didn't.

She knew he hadn't wanted to be seen touching her so intimately. He as much as showed her that he couldn't be counted on when anyone else was around. His boots clomped off the bridge and down the subtly lit commonway. His reaction practically drove her right into Sean's drunken arms. David's jealousy rose in a fast wave. He planned to straighten a few things out, starting right now.

Mari's suite came up on his left, but he passed right by it. His target waited a little ways down on the right.

He pressed the sensor to Sean's door several times, barely allowing the faint echo of the chime to fade before triggering it again in his impatience. For a moment, his mind wandered to thoughts he wouldn't fully let manifest about Sean being somewhere else right now. He looked down toward Mari's suite and his whole body tensed. David contacted Sean's reporter directly. "Open up, Sean."

Sean's look was not welcoming when the metal door slid open. In fact, David sensed more than their usual tension, as if the mech tech were prepared for a fight like David had been just a few seconds ago. Sean Cryer definitely had Armadan aggressor genes inside him.

"What do you want?" Sean asked.

"What I *don't* want is to discuss this in the commonway."

Sean moved aside, his rigid posture slightly threatening. He was only a few centimeters shorter than David, and though his frame was medium-sized, his shoulders were broad and his muscles taut and ropy. David could tell when a man was spoiling for a fight, and Sean was ready to throw down the minute David gave him a reason.

"Would you relax?" David said. "I came to make sure you got the money I transferred into your account."

Sean checked the blue glow of data scrolling across his palm. "Why did you do this?"

"That's the money Mari owes you."

"I told her she didn't have to pay me back."

"*She's* not paying you back. *I am*," David said. "And her rent is paid up for a year now, so you don't have to worry about spotting her again. I would appreciate it if you kept this between us. I don't know what kind of relationship the two of—"

"She's a colleague and a friend," Sean said, agitation creeping into his voice. "Nothing more. Never was. Never will be."

David studied Sean's face, but all he saw were bloodshot eyes with dark circles underneath them and a weariness that was unexpected for his young years. David relaxed a little. Sean obviously had his own problems, and though he might be secretive about most of his life, he had no reason to lie to David about Mari.

Sean regarded him for a moment. "By the way, I asked around about Mari's client. Couldn't find much."

David nodded his head. So it had simply been David's jealousy convincing him there was something wrong with Dale, aside from a poor taste in scentbots and a penchant for roving hands.

"Then I owe Mari an apology. At least there's nothing to worry about, I guess."

"I don't think you understand what I'm saying," Sean said. "His file is a little too clean. Much of it isn't even public, which means he's got an Embassy protector keeping things tidy. Maybe you could use your military connections to find out more."

"Thanks." David's protective instincts engaged again as Sean practically confirmed the bittersweet truth that Dale was hiding something. "I appreciate it."

"Is Mari in trouble?" Sean asked.

"I hope not," David muttered as he left.

Good thing Ben stayed in the fleet.

David had four brothers. Ben was the middle one, therefore also the loudest, most talkative, and probably the most personable of them all. Though Colin was in between them, David and Ben were always closer because Colin had no interest in the Armada, choosing to become a civilian engineer instead. Ben, on the other hand, may have been even more gung ho about the military than David, or maybe because of David, wanting to be just like his big brother. But instead of following in David's footsteps, Ben joined a special operations unit which moved around within the fleet, never sticking to a steady rise in rank aboard a particular ship, like David had with the *Protector*.

That gave Ben, as a simple lieutenant, access to more classified channels than David ever had as a captain.

When Ben's familiar grin and dark brows appeared on the airscreen, David was struck by how much he and Ben were starting to look alike the older they got, even though many people didn't think so. With only seven years separating them, David thought Ben still seemed much younger.

"I need some information on a guy named Dale Zapona," David said.

"Oh, I see how it is. Use me and abuse me, but don't call just to say hello."

"Hello, Ben," David said. "Can you do a background check on Dale Zapona?"

"Of course. And while I'm doing the search, maybe you can tell me how your run-in with that asshole Killian Doje went, or better yet, who you've been docking. Because word has it you were seen last night kissing a little blonde Socialite along the boardwalk on Carrey Bay."

To prove his point, Ben replaced his image with a vid. It was of David and Mari's kiss.

"Or was she just someone you met that night? How old is she? Her Embassy file said nineteen, but I can't imagine you with a teenager, even one who looked like that."

"*She's* none of your business, Ben." David's tone was light, but held a subtle warning. "How do you even know about her? Or Killian?"

Ben's image flicked back on screen.

"Your romantic interlude got picked up by a voyeur just like your reunion with Killian. I have an alert on all the family in case anyone's in trouble."

"Or because you're a bigger gossip than half the Socialites in this system," David said.

"Come on, I can see not wanting to talk about the asshole, but give me some info on the blonde. What's her name?"

"Like you don't already know," David muttered.

"Boston. Sweet name. But you called her Mari when you said she was beautiful." Ben could barely contain his glee. *"Why is that?"*

"Why do you bother to ask questions you know the answers to?"

"Just making conversation. You know, I haven't seen you kiss anyone like that since Lyra, though you do seem to have a thing for blondes with tight asses. And in that little blue dress that Bos—that Mari was wearing, it was pretty easy to see her—"

"At least I have a personal life. Do you even remember the name of the last woman you docked?" David asked.

That actually silenced Ben, and David wished he could have taken the comment back, sensing Ben must have been sensitive about the topic. They hadn't talked in months, but he knew Ben better than any person in the system. When he got quiet, something was wrong. Kind of like Mari.

"What's up?" David asked.

"Besides your dick?"

Ben joked because he didn't want to talk about whatever was bothering him, so David let his inquiry drop.

"Anyway, what are you willing to pay for this classified information?" Ben leaned on his forearms, bringing his face closer to the camera conspiratorially.

"What do you want?" David knew it would be something absurd because Ben was all about helping out family. He'd do anything David asked, including fly a gunship straight into a star.

"I want the operating codes to your boat next time I have leave."

"You have a boat."

"I had a boat…that was in a little accident last month."

"I'll send you the codes as long as you promise there won't be any *accidents*, little or otherwise."

"I only make promises I can keep, David. I thought Mum taught you that, too."

"Your emotional blackmail will only get you so far," David said.

"In this guilt-ridden family? It gets me everything and anything."

That was certainly a true statement, though an ironic one considering Ben was the most susceptible to guilt out of them all.

"I'll get back to you as soon as the background check comes in on your guy."

"Thanks, Ben."

Ben flipped him off with a laugh before his image blinked off.

David was probably over-reacting. If there turned out to be a problem with Dale's background, David would explain it to Mari. She'd drop out of the project and he'd help her find another client. Simple.

If she didn't believe him, he could always make up an excuse to get the *Bard* in the sky and away from the Hub until Mari could talk with Ben herself. Surely it wouldn't come to that kind of subterfuge, but Mari had been pretty upset earlier. And David would do whatever it took to keep her safe, even if she hated him for it and he lost his chance to be with her.

"I messed up, didn't I?" Mari pushed the heap of clothes from Sean's sofa onto the floor and slumped down on the worn white cushions.

"Those were clean," Sean said.

"Really? They looked kind of wrinkled."

Sean was about to take a bite of a sandwich, but Mari looked at it expectantly. "Is that peanut butter?"

Sean ripped the sandwich apart and gave her half.

"Thanks," she said. "Nothing tastes as good as peanut butter, except peanut butter with some sugar sprinkled on top or dipped in syrup."

Sean popped the rest of his sandwich in his mouth.

"Did you eat that already?" She said through the peanut butter clinging to the roof of her mouth.

"Half a sandwich takes half the time to eat," Sean said.

She couldn't even muster a laugh, just a small, sad smile.

"Can I have a drink of that?"

Sean passed her the bottle of water he held to his lips.

She took a big swig and offered it back, but Sean waved her off.

"I shouldn't have lost my temper," she said. "He just made me so mad. Do you know how frustrating he can be? And did you notice he's a little bossy?"

"All the time," Sean said.

"But I like him." She swirled the remaining water around in the clear bottle, watching it bubble and slosh like it was confused and crashing in on itself. That's how she felt, like a crash was imminent. "He was my first, you know. My *only*."

A long silence drifted into the room.

Sean shifted uncomfortably. "Look, I don't really want to get involved, but things might not be as bad with David as you think."

Her head snapped up. "What do you mean?"

"I *mean*, have you talked to him recently?"

"Since when?" she asked.

"Since you implied you and I were going to have sex?"

Her face flushed hot. "I wasn't implying that."

"Yeah, you were. You wanted to see if he'd take my head off. A little while ago I thought he might try it."

Mari sat up in alarm. "David came here to confront you? Are you okay? I shouldn't have put you in danger. That was irresponsible. He could have killed you or broken your arms and legs at the least."

"Wait a minute." Sean held up a hand to silence her. "Why do you assume he would have won?"

Mari did laugh this time, a small, reflexive giggle that jumped right out of her mouth before she could shut it again.

Sean's look was anything but amused.

"It's just that..."

Because I saw him take on six guys, two of whom were as big as you?

"...he's been military trained. You're just a scientist."

"I'm not just a—never mind." Sean shook his head like he wanted to say more about it, but decided not to. He took a deep breath. "Just because he looks bigger doesn't necessarily mean he's better in a fight."

"I didn't mean any offense, Sean. You're still tougher than everyone else on this ship, including me."

It was a compliment, but the indignant groan rumbling through Sean's chest said he hadn't taken it as one.

"David paid your rent and paid me back for those months I spotted you. So go thank him and put this bullshit behind you and make sure you let him know that I was the one who told you all this because I told him I wouldn't."

Mari's heart thudded with the news. A million emotions passed through her at once from disbelief to embarrassment and finally to pure joy. She leaped off the couch and threw her arms around Sean. He gave her a little hug back.

"For the record," he said. "I could take him."

The look in his eyes made her wonder if that could be true.

"Maybe." She kissed him on the cheek and bounded out of the room, then peeked back in to say, "But I doubt it."

"I'm not going to take the job." Mari stood in the entrance to the bridge, her arms and their contents tucked neatly behind her.

David spun in the nav chair to face her. Though his expression was mostly unreadable, she didn't detect any sign of anger.

"I stopped by your suite, but you weren't there," she said. "What are you doing in here? We aren't in danger of crashing into the dock, are we?" she joked.

"I haven't crashed into a dock since flight training. I have scars from that, too, but only on my ego." He smiled at her.

She liked his good nature.

"What made you change your mind?" he asked.

"You were right," she said. "I don't think Dale was only looking at my resume when he wanted to hire me." She studied the shiny black floor.

"That's his problem, not yours. You understand that, don't you?"

She gave a pathetic little nod.

"You're smart, Mari, and enthusiastic, and you have drive. Look at what you've accomplished on your own at such a young age. And, don't give me that *I'm almost twenty* line because you should be proud of doing all this by yourself as a teenager."

"You helped. That's why I brought this to thank you." She pulled the bottle of Koley's from behind her back and set it on the crash couch.

He looked at it a bit suspiciously. "Not that I'm in the habit of turning down bourbon, but *thank me* for what?"

"For paying my rent. And reimbursing Sean. I promise to pay you back for all of it…eventually."

"It was a gift, supposed to be an *anonymous* gift, so you wouldn't have to worry about paying anyone back and just concentrate on your career for a while, but I can guess who told you."

"Sean did. Just now."

"Sean has a big mouth," David said.

"Yes, he does, but it's not as nice as yours."

Mari put her hands on David's shoulders and straddled him in the nav chair. He didn't protest, even with the bridge door open wide to the commonway. She stared into his grey eyes and thought she read a hopeful expectation there.

He rested his hands on her hips, and she felt the warmth of his touch spread through the rest of her body. Leaning in, she kissed him—a little more urgently than she meant to. He responded in kind, sweeping her chest against him. She inhaled his scent and marveled at how much she missed this small intimacy. When she pulled away, it was only so she could see his face again. He had a kind and handsome face with small lines beginning to crease the corners of his eyes and mouth. That meant he had smiled a lot over his life so far. She wanted those same lines someday.

"I'm sorry, Mari." His expression became serious.

"I'm the one here trying to apologize." She smoothed a finger over his thick brows.

She was going to tell him more, but he stole her thoughts as he kissed the divot above her clavicle. All the tension left her body, replaced by the bliss of David's touch. Mari pressed into his hips, delighting in his hardness. When he grabbed her backside and rocked her against him, waves of heat pooled between her legs.

"Can we do what we did last night?" she whispered in his ear.

"I'd like that," he said.

"And maybe we could try something new, too."

"New is good." He was already sliding her little tank top up over her belly.

She heard the bridge door snap closed. He did like his privacy.

Filling out reports is a waste of time.

David sent his meticulously detailed incident report to his private files via his reporter as he left the air conditioning of the contractors' guild. He should have felt relieved, but he suspected Killian had his own motives for not including David or Mari in the official Embassy report. There was bound to be more trouble to come.

Maybe he should count them lucky. It would seem luck was in his favor recently, most of it centering on his new relationship with Mari. After their *apologies* on the bridge, she and David had had dinner in his suite, where they talked and laughed just like they always had. His constant caresses convinced her to stay the night.

He covered a yawn that turned into a smile. Sleep wasn't a high priority last night, but he'd take the tiredness every day to have Mari all night, every night.

David's reporter vibrated against his skin, signaling an incoming transmission. He eddied out of the flow of pedestrian traffic heading into the government building, hoping it was Mari saying she was on her way back already. He was hesitant for her to go to Dale's estate alone, even if it was to tell him she wasn't taking his project. After their argument and his behavior in Dale's presence last time, David understood her wanting to do this on her own. Personally, he felt a nice message sent from the *Bard* would have sufficed, but Mari insisted she handle this in person as it was the professional way to respond. It was all over now, though, and within a few hours they'd be lifting off from Tampa Quad, on their way to pick up Geir.

An Armadan insignia flashed across the blue screen projected onto his palm with *UNCLASSIFIED: CIVILIAN TRANSMISSION* scrolling across Ben's signature. It was an odd reminder of David's new place in life.

"Hey, Ben. I thought I'd hear back from you yesterday. Big night?" David asked.

"Yes, but not in the way you think. I started following background trails for your guy Zapona. It took me a while to find out just how big a cocksucker he is."

David didn't like the sound of this already.

"He's a real sleazy son of a bitch. Has ties to a suspected crime boss psychopath named Liu Stavros." Ben paused, tension working at his jaw. *"This doesn't have anything to do with Mari, does it?"*

David could tell by the worry in Ben's expression that he wasn't trying to make a joke.

"Why?"

"Because fleet intelligence has a special alert out for Liu Stavros. Though we can't get past the Embassy firewalls on this one, it's suspected in intelligence circles that Stavros is into human trafficking. Sex crimes. Mutilation. Torture. All the victims were purported to be young women, almost exclusively from Deleine, all with the same distinctive genetic mutation."

"Coral-colored eyes." Anger burned through David. "What is the guy still doing walking around?"

"Beats the shit out of me, except that every case against him has disappeared from public record. And so has Stavros for that matter. Guy's a recluse."

"Probably has an Embassy insider doing his cover-ups. Maybe using intimidation?" David asked.

"Or a payoff, but there would have to be some pretty heavy funds to keep someone, or several someones, quiet about rape and murder."

David agreed. Especially about the rape. Sexual crimes were often dealt with more severely than murder simply because their society relied so much on the safety of sexual freedom. Not to mention the stigma attached to forcing oneself upon an unwilling partner when millions were available. Having so many choices was one of the perks of multi-partner marriage, though many Armadans still subscribed to monogamy.

"It gets better. Eight months ago a covert fleet team pursued a lead to Stavros's supplier in the trafficking trade, only the trail went dead when the local Embassy officials were contacted. None of the team made it back. Job got botched at an undisclosed location on Tampa Deux. Command error was the official response, but everyone following that op knows that's bullshit. Someone leaked details to Stavros. Want to guess who the suspected supplier was?"

"Dale." Alarms went off inside David's head.

"I take it by that look of rage on your face this is bad news."

"Mari's on her way to see him right now." The thought of her in a room alone with Dale had David's blood boiling.

"You need any help with this fucker, fleet-sanctioned or otherwise, just say the word."

Before Ben's image even blinked out, David was already calling Mari's reporter. Her messaging service picked up.

"Mari, head back to the *Bard* immediately. If you're still at Dale's, tell him there's been an emergency. And message me when you're on your way. I don't want to scare you, but I believe you're in danger."

"Were you in the military?" Mari asked Carlos, trying to make small talk as he escorted her through the gate with that horrible tree emblazoned on it.

The question awarded her a glare, sending a shiver down her spine. This guy was as big as David, yet David's size had never intimidated her, only made her feel secure. Carlos's imposing frame had the exact opposite effect. She wanted to turn right around and call Dale safely from the other side of his gate.

Her finger absently touched her palm, hoping David may have left her an encouraging message, but nothing happened. When she saw her bare wrist, a sick feeling of vulnerability trickled into her chest.

"I forgot...." She had been so distracted this morning.

Carlos stopped and regarded her. "Forgot what?"

"Nothing." For some reason, she didn't want him to know she was walking in here without her reporter. Maybe because she felt cut off from the outside world or because she was about to face a man she believed had ulterior motives. Suddenly today felt bleak, despite the beautiful weather.

Amidst a backdrop of fern trees, Dale sat at a lavishly set table with brilliant white linens, silver trays, and turquoise china plates. He smiled as she approached. She wondered how long that smile would last once she turned him down.

"Good morning, dear. Would you like something?"

"No, thank you. I had breakfast already." She had made crepes for David this morning—her thanks for the pasta he'd prepared for her last night. The thought of David brought back her nerve.

"Not even a celebratory mimosa?" Dale held up a thin-stemmed glass with a pale orange liquid. "It reminds me of your eyes a bit."

91

Mari didn't like the way he said that part about her eyes. She tried a quick smile anyway, to hide her anxiety. "Sorry. No. I really just came by to say thank you for the job offer."

"You're quite welcome." He made a gesture of looking all around her. "No luggage?"

"I won't be needing any—"

"Because you're not going to accept the offer," Dale said, putting his celebratory glass down.

"I'm sorry," she said.

"I'm disappointed."

She forced herself to keep his gaze as she shifted her weight from one foot to the other, aware of how her toes scrunched in the high heels. "Now's just not the best time…." She really didn't have any excuses and hadn't planned to give any. In fact, she had anticipated giving her regrets, then high-tailing it back to the *Bard*. The longer she stood in Dale's presence, the more she considered running out the gate.

"I understand, dear." His casual manner as he finished his breakfast put her at ease a bit. He was taking her rejection better than she could have hoped.

"That's a relief. Please keep me in mind for any future projects," she said, wondering if she should add, *unless I have to be on a freighter for six weeks*, but decided to keep quiet about that.

Dale finished his mimosa. Mari guessed he wasn't going to say more because there was no way he would consider her to be even a grounds keeper after this.

"Tell me, was your decision influenced by your pilot?"

"David? Well, not really."

"I think we know better than that. It's a shame, but I can see he wouldn't want you wandering too far away. Men are so selfish sometimes. Armadans terribly so. The older they get, the more possessive they become." He tsked as though pitying her.

A touch of anger burned on Mari's cheeks. She opened her mouth to defend her decision, but his next words stopped her.

"Maybe *David* won't mind if you designed my hydroponics bay from your own ship. That way he can keep an eye on you," Dale said.

The modified offer sparked a new hope inside her.

"Are you asking me to still be a part of the greenshift project? To work from the *Bard*?" She wanted to be clear about this last part because it was an offer she would have never expected.

"It would seem I have no choice if I want your expertise."

Her mind raced. It was a perfect solution.

"Though I do request that you look over the facilities on the *Thrall 7* before it leaves this morning. We can go there first, then I'll have the driver drop you at your own berth."

She hesitated at this request, but kept thinking about the look Dale had given her earlier when he thought David had so much control over her. That's why she had left home to begin with—she wanted to control her own path.

"What do you say, Mari? Do we have an accord?"

"Let's go see the *Thrall*," she said.

"He drives a little fast, doesn't he?" Mari said.

Dale gave her an amused look as he sat across from her in the back of his personal transport. He lounged with one knee crossed over the other and his arm sprawled along the back of the tan leather seat.

Mari had pressed into a corner and tried not to fidget, pretending Dale no longer made her nervous now that they had come to an agreement. She reminded herself how this would get her out of debt, allow her to pay David back, and make her resume as good as Dale thought it was. Plus, his recommendations to other greenshift customers could mean a sustained career for as long as she wanted. She could become as rich as Soli and Kenon and wear expensive clothes and eat at nice places like the Rose of Sharon all the time.

And maybe move her family off Deleine, if they would go. She hadn't heard from any of them since landing at the Hub. Out of habit she touched her palm to check messages. *Dammit!*

"Dale, I'm sorry. You'll have to send me the specs from the ship later." Mari held up her naked wrist. "I didn't wear my reporter this morning." She hoped she didn't come off as being absent-minded. Sean was always reminding her to keep the device on or splurge for an implant.

"Of course," Dale said. "You can point out specifics during our tour of the vessel, and I'll make sure you receive all the information you require."

As they passed the ferry station, en route to the other side of Shiraz Dock, a mocha-skinned woman in a short, pink sari caught Mari's attention through the transport's window. Soli looked up just in time to see Mari drive by. She thought of giving her shipmate a little wave, but they were already past. Seeing Soli heading back to the *Bard* cheered Mari. The *Bard* was home, and this job made it possible for her to stay there…with David.

She imagined her nights being just like last night and her mornings just like this morning. Then her daydreams turned to images of visiting David's home on Yurai, having him show her the mountains and the lake. She became lost in her thoughts, content with fantasizing about a new, bright future.

"If you like the sight of a freighter that much, dear, then you should reconsider joining us during this voyage," Dale said.

"Oh, no, I mean I was thinking about…it's impressive." It was really quite ugly, but most freighters were, especially compared to the graceful, silver curves of the *Bard*.

As they exited the transport, Carlos kept mimicking that sweeping stare that she had witnessed David perform at Dale's estate, as though he expected something to pop out and attack. Must have been a military habit. It unnerved her. So did Dale's proximity as he escorted her toward the *Thrall*'s gangway. As she picked her way along the metal grating, sallow light flickered in the metal tube like an eclipsing sun. She couldn't see past the darkness at the other end to gauge anything about the ship's interior.

An oxidizing scent enveloped her, reminding her of wet metal. It could have been from automatic cleaners built into the ship's ceiling like sprinklers. Though programmable domestics might be more convenient than bringing in a cleaning crew like the *Bard* did every few months, the effects couldn't be as sanitary.

A catwalk ran overhead, following their progress through the dim commonway. A series of pipes snaked beneath, reminding Mari that the ship was a lot like a plant—food from the roots was transported throughout the vessel via tubes. Although the *Thrall* didn't have that feeling of life running in its veins, so maybe it was more of a dying husk. The nutrients, the water were all there, but no vitality, no color.

They passed a couple of men in coveralls. The leering stares of the laborers stood her hair on end. She rubbed her bare arms, wishing she would have worn a top that covered a little more, and not just because of the chill inside the ship.

"Do you have many passengers on the *Thrall*?" she asked.

"We have crew, not passengers," Dale said. "Seventy-five, though most of them either work in the lower decks or wait there until we're ready to off-load or take on cargo."

"There are only six of us on the *Bard*. How does everyone fit here?" Granted the *Thrall* was twice as big as Mari's ship, but with the cargo bays comprising the bulk of the vessel, crew quarters had to be packed tight.

"We make room when we need it," Dale said, adding a note of finality to the chitchat.

Her eyes adjusted to the scant light seeping from runners along the commonway's floor, but the dreariness inside this ship pressed around her small form. So did Carlos. He'd shadowed her more closely with each step the farther they moved into the ship. Occasionally his arm brushed her shoulder. She wanted to shrink away from him, but there was nowhere to go.

At least the visit would be over within the hour. The thought of living here on the *Thrall* for six months was depressing at best, horrifying at worst. What had she been thinking?

Their shoes tapped a muted cadence along the hard rubber floor. Carlos's heavy steps nearly vibrated up her leg. Needing to take some control, she slowed her pace, forcing Carlos to back off ever so slightly. She was about to ask for a little more room when she spotted the filtration system running along the wall to their right. Only advanced hydroponics labs had that kind of system, and judging by the slight organic smell and humming condensers, this one was already operational. Why would Dale need her if he had a system in place? Perhaps this one needed to be adjusted. But, Dale specifically wanted a system designed from scratch. He could just be ripping this one out entirely and starting over...which would be astronomically expensive.

Little jolts of foreboding swept through her fingers, and the hairs on the back of her neck stood up as David's concerns jabbed into her mind. When Carlos's hand touched her shoulder to guide her toward a corridor on the left, she screamed.

Her echoed cry startled Dale, making him whip around. "You frighten too easily, dear."

She was definitely frightened.

"I just don't like people touching me," she said. *Specifically him*, she wanted to add.

"That could be a problem for you later," Dale said, more to himself than Mari.

Still she didn't like the way he said it. Or the way he led them away from the hydroponics bay. Her heart raced. A rush of panic rolled through her chest and surged out into her limbs in little adrenaline licks of electricity.

Carlos's body blocked her exit back to the gangway. If she could just get around his huge bulk. Refusing to take another step away from escape, Mari stopped and grabbed at her ear, snatching the silver hoop out.

"I think I dropped my earring." She ducked down and acted as though she were searching the floor. "Can you help me find it?"

Dale grumbled.

"Sorry, but they were a gift." Mari stealthily maneuvered around the Armadan's leg.

"Fine. Help her," Dale said.

As soon as Carlos stooped over, Mari casually slid her body around him. Then she bolted for the gangway.

Keep it calm. Mari hasn't been gone that long.

David didn't even make it up the *Bard*'s gangway before Sean met him. Maybe he had news. He hadn't when David contacted him from the contractors' guild.

"Found Mari's reporter in her room." Sean held up the small silver bracelet. "She must have forgotten it this morning. She does that sometimes. There was another message on there besides yours…from Dale." Sean's voice tightened saying the man's name.

He played the audio for David.

"I'm sorry I missed you today, dear. I thought you were planning to come by this morning, but I suppose you not showing up is your answer. Such a shame. It would have been nice to work with you. Maybe some other time."

"Bullshit," David said. "He's lying, covering his tracks."

"That's what I figure, too," Sean said.

"I'm heading over to get Mari now," David said.

"At the industrial docks?" Solimar Robbins sauntered up the gangway in a revealing pink sari that showed off her shapely legs and her Upper Caste poise. Few women David had met had her grace or her penchant for being in other people's business.

"What are you talking about?" David asked.

"I just saw Mari leaving Wright's Landing. She was in the back of a high-end transport heading toward the commercial side of the docks."

David looked at Sean. "That's where the *Thrall* would be berthed. If he takes her on board…." Anger and panic wouldn't let David finish his thought.

"It'll take forever to get across the bay on a ferry," Sean said.

"How else are we going to get there?"

"A municipal fast track."

"Do you plan on stealing one from the dock officials?" David needed *feasible* ideas. Sure the lightweight, high speed mini boats could cover the distance from one dock to the other in one tenth of the time a passenger ferry could, but he didn't have access to one.

"It's easier than you think," Sean said.

David's head snapped around, his hope pushing out thoughts of committing a felony. "Then do it. In the meantime, Soli, can you use your archivist credentials to track that transport to its destination?"

"I'll try to access the stationary cameras along their route, and maybe syphon something from any voyeurs wandering around, but I can't promise much."

"Send us anything you get," David said. "No matter how small."

"Is Mari okay?" she asked.

David didn't wait to respond—he and Sean ran for the municipal docks. Dodging pedestrians along the concrete boardwalk, the two men drew more than a few grumbles of displeasure. When a group of Embassy office staffers froze in David's path, he shouldered through their grey suited figures without a word of apology. He dove into combat mode and focused on his mission—get to Mari.

To his surprise, Sean matched him stride for stride. David had assumed the mech tech's sedentary lifestyle wouldn't include conditioning, but Sean was almost in military-grade shape.

The communications barbican curved into view ahead, appearing like a great concrete and glass ship about to take flight. This red and black, multi-leveled structure monitored traffic for all three docks surrounding Carrey Bay. It also was the sole point of access to the municipal docks from the domestic berths.

David slowed his pace as the security gate came into view. The blue glimmer of an electronic barrier funneled visitors through two scanners. If he and Sean were to reach the restricted municipal area, they'd have to make it through those scanners, like the hundred or so other citizens already in the queue.

"If we wait in that line we'll never make it," Sean said.

"We're not waiting in line." David shouldered his way amongst the crowd, Sean on his heels.

A group of dock workers formed a blockade, intent on not letting them pass. But David moved them with a stare, the resentment from last night's attack most likely written all over his face. These men weren't the same ones who had assaulted him and Mari, but they reminded him too much of them.

As he came closer to the automated gate sensor, he hung back a bit in line. Pungent smells of sulfides and petrol-based substances mixed with the scent of bodies standing too close in the stagnant air surrounding the entrance. A concrete wave of a wall blocked the sea breezes, forming an eddy of heat and trapping the miasma of chemical and organic scents. It agitated David, heightening his unpleasant mood. He shoved farther up the line.

Just two laborers remained between David and entry. "Do we rush the gate when these guys go in?" he asked Sean.

"Ever jump one of these before?" Sean countered.

"No."

"If the sensor detects more than one person entering, it triggers an alarm and locks both offenders in between this gate and the next one."

David wondered at the secondary access just a few meters from the first. Now it made sense, like opposite ends of a steel cage.

"Watch," Sean said.

One of the men in front of them slid his wrist over a waist-high scanner within a concrete column that followed the exact curve of the entire barbican. The man's worn reporter looked clunky and hopelessly outdated compared to the one Sean had provided for David, but the antiquated equipment did the job—both gates dropped their electronic shields at the same time, allowing him access through each one in turn.

David looked to Sean for their next step.

"We're going to trick the sensor," Sean said.

"How?"

"I have a hack that will mimic the algorithm used by that last guy's reporter."

"Won't it register that he went through already?" David asked.

"Believe it or not, the security system doesn't care how many times the same ident goes through, just so it's one of the ones programmed for this area."

"I hope you're right," David said.

"I am. You're up first." Sean held his naked wrist over the gate sensor.

Prompted by his implanted reporter, lines of coded gibberish flew across the blue screen projected onto his palm. Within seconds Sean's hack opened both electronic gates. David forced a casual pace into the *cage*, but he was ready to sprint for the other gate if he heard an alarm. Halfway there he fought the urge to bolt. He balled his fists and tensed his arms as if to come out swinging, but there wouldn't be anything he could do against an electronic gate.

Two more steps and he passed beyond the second scanner. The shield glimmered back to life momentarily until Sean tricked the sensor again. Though he made it look easy, David could only imagine how sophisticated the program was which allowed them access to such a secure area.

David's reporter vibrated. "Did you find them, Soli?"

"Yes, according to several dockside cameras, her transport arrived at berth six-two-four. She entered a freighter with two men. She seemed nervous, David."

Soli's voice quivered, whether out of true concern or melodrama, David wouldn't speculate.

"Keep an eye on that freighter. If you see any activity, like Mari leaving, let us know."

David knew Soli wouldn't see any such thing.

"This way," Sean said.

They mingled with some of the dock workers until they could break off and head toward the fast track slips.

Sean kept his voice low and asked, "Are you going to tell me what's going on before we get there?"

"Dale is part of a human trafficking ring. Apparently, some sick asshole has a thing for raping Deleinean women, then killing them."

For the first time David saw a flicker of concern cross Sean's face, but the mech tech remained silent.

"Maybe I should have contacted the authorities," David said.

"Because they were so helpful the last two times you encountered them?" Sean asked. "I wouldn't trust the contractors' guild here with Mari's life, and if what we suspect is true about Dale, he's had a man on the inside covering up his shit for so long that nothing is going to stick to him now."

Sean suddenly motioned David back behind a massive support pillar. A maintenance woman strode within a few meters of them, but never looked up from the data on her palm. As soon as she moved into another section of the shipyard, David and Sean headed straight to the nearest slip.

The smell of the salt water usurped all other smells, its freshness invigorating David as they took the next step to completing their mission. He had to keep thinking of

Mari in such a way, otherwise his emotions threatened to paralyze him and steal his ability to strategize. She had come to mean so much to him over the past month, and he would be damned if Dale Zapona was going to take her away from him.

"Can you drive one of these things?" Sean asked.

"Yeah." David's boat back home was similar to the fast track.

"Then get ready to move out as soon as I disable the slip's electro-magnetic leash."

"Better do it fast," David said, jumping into the speed boat and engaging the starter. A brief glance over the controls made him confident he could handle the craft in open water—he'd powered up and down Cheat Lake hundreds of times.

"Move," Sean said.

David pushed the throttle full tilt, kicking up a blinding spray and throwing Sean to the floor as they jumped away from the slip.

"Shit," Sean said.

"Thought you'd know to hold on," David said as Sean stumbled to stand beside him at the controls.

Squinting against the salty wind, David assessed the water traffic zigzagging ahead. The ferries had the right of way in every instance, but since they had their own lanes, he wasn't worried as much about them as the smaller commercial craft. He'd skirt the closest ones and make a straight path to the industrial docks. Hopefully even the larger commercial shuttles would give way to an official craft.

You'll get her back.

David battled to control his emotions with each minute that slipped by. But his concentration waivered as he spun the fast track away from an oncoming shuttle at the last minute. He received a blast from their horn in reprimand. At least the tinted fishbowl cover hid the angry expressions of whoever rode inside.

Keep it together.

Traffic thinned as the fast track approached the industrial docks. Even as the boat skipped across the small waves of the bay, the trip felt excruciatingly slow. Dale had a head start on them. Plus, the *Thrall* would have already been prepped for departure this morning.

David scanned the dock area. "You see a spot close to the six hundred block of berths?"

"I don't even see any signs coming in from this side," Sean said.

Neither did David so he headed for the nearest slip.

He killed the throttle at the last minute, bumping the fast track into the slot without any of the finesse the sleek boat deserved. Both men hit the dock and bolted. Onlookers jumped out of their way as David and Sean pushed past. Once inside the main flow of pedestrian traffic, they stopped for a moment, confused as the docks split off in a half moon with six different spokes leading to hundreds of huge berths.

This industrial side of Shiraz looked like its own city, some of the larger space-faring ships looming so high they created pockets of dark shadows along the boardwalk. It was intimidating in its immensity—lights flashed in a spectrum of colors from ships all around them, signaling various stages of docking or launching, and the noise level was nearly deafening. Exhaust fumes wafted over them from several faulty converters as David cast a glance over the signs.

"Six hundred block is this way." Sean took off down the closest boardwalk.

Each time an in-atmosphere engine roared to life, David's heart stuttered. He watched each ship slowly drift out over the open water, clear of the docks and ferries, until they could safely engage their break away engines and punch out of the atmosphere. Each ignition flare made him realize that Mari was already too far away. His only relief came from knowing the *Bard* was a faster ship than the *Thrall*.

They came up on berth six-one-seven when David spotted four contractors on patrol ahead. Maybe he should enlist the authorities' help after all. He almost changed course when he saw the third cender strapped to one contractor's thigh.

Killian zeroed in on David before he could duck away.

David gave Sean's arm a small punch. "This way. Company up ahead."

They veered around a towering science vessel—the real kind, not what the *Bard* pretended to be. Multiple antenna arrays and in-atmosphere vents bristled along the ship's black metal shell, casting shadowy quills along the stained concrete. David and Sean wove around the reinforced titanium beast.

Though the docks would connect on the other side, David wanted to move past one more berth in case Killian or the others had decided to cut them off. He led Sean between a cargo loader's huge claw, which sported only a smudge of its original yellow paint, and the dingy freighter it was unloading. This should be far enough from their original position to merge back into dock traffic.

There was only one more freighter left. It had to be the *Thrall 7*. David's heart sped up with hope. Then he saw the bright glow of warming engines. The ship could make its run for the lift-off area any time.

He broke cover. The quickest way to Mari was straight down the main pedestrian thoroughfare. He could deal with Killian later.

David felt the hairs on his arms and on the back of his neck stand on end and try to pull away from his skin. Only one thing caused that dreadful sensation.

"Cender!"

He and Sean dove for cover behind a weathered cargo container, but the concentrated bolt of static electricity caught David across the back, scorching his shirt and a strip of skin underneath.

"What the hell?" Sean asked.

"That little shit Ward is scratching an itch." David barely felt the burn on his back as he heard the *Thrall*'s secondary engines whine into high gear, the last stage of pre-flight.

"Get away from me." Mari's panicked voice echoed around the metallic walls of the commonway as big hands grasped her forearm and yanked her back hard.

Carlos dragged her away from any possible escape. The freighter shook as the engines powered higher—they were going to take off.

She pounded her fist against Carlos's biceps and pulled at his thick fingers to free herself, but it was like fighting a boulder. She kicked at his leg, managed to lose her balance and fell. He never stopped, banging her knees off the floor and rubbing away the skin on her ankles. She lost her shoes in the scramble to regain her footing.

"Let go of me. Someone help me! Please."

Trying a new approach, she grabbed at the corrugated walls, but the metal only sliced into her fingers as Carlos continued unimpeded. Out of desperation, she threw her foot in front of his, tripping him. He stumbled but didn't go down. Jerking her toward him, he slammed her against the wall so hard her teeth shook. The cold steel sucked the warmth from her body.

Mari couldn't speak, couldn't scream, just stared into Carlos's hazel eyes, trying to see a glimmer of mercy.

"Don't be stupid, you freaky-eyed bitch," Carlos said. "We're in the last stages of takeoff. You'd never be able to breach that seal if you tried. All you're doing is hurting yourself and making me look like a fool." His grip tightened around her shoulders, his fingers pushing into her muscles until she wanted to cry. "I won't play the fool for anyone."

He slammed her into the wall again, then dropped her. The hard rubber surface stung against the balls of her bare feet.

"What are you going to do with me?" she asked, hating the dread she heard in her own voice.

Carlos snatched her by the back of the neck and jostled her ahead.

Dale waited for them where her failed escape attempt began. She didn't expect him to give her any more answers than Carlos, but she needed to ask.

"What are you going to do with me?"

"We're going to strap you in for takeoff." He motioned for Carlos to drive her forward again.

"Why are you doing this? I don't want to be here with you. I don't want anything to do with you."

Dale gave a harsh laugh. "And you think I want anything to do with you? I can have any woman I want. There's nothing that interests me about you except that some rich psychopath is willing to pay for a Deleinean woman with orange eyes."

"My eyes aren't orange." The snip surprised her. She had had to deal with insults and teasing all her life. The defensiveness from childhood bullying came back easily, almost involuntarily.

"Well, whatever color you want to call them, they're not natural."

That's how Dale looked at her, like some diseased mongrel, even though her blood was as pure Upper Caste as his. But if her genes had been strong, he would reason, her eyes wouldn't have changed.

"To my client, your un-natural state makes you an oddity. He collects oddities, uses them, destroys them for his own pleasure. And do you know what he does to women with orange eyes?"

"What?" Mari asked in a whisper.

"He plucks them right out of their heads."

She couldn't process what Dale was saying. This wasn't real. She was having a nightmare. All she needed to do was wake up and David would be sleeping right beside her. She could curl up next to him, and he'd make this horrible dream go away.

Reality crashed down upon her as Carlos pushed her toward an open door on their left where a crash couch waited.

"Who's this guy you're talking about? Why would he want to do that to me? Please tell me where we're going," she shouted.

Panic overtook her. As soon as Carlos loosened his grip, she twisted free and pummeled Dale in the head. Drawing her arm back, she punched him in the nose, sending a blast of pain through her knuckles. Dale recoiled, covering his face. She rained blow after blow on his head, fighting like a wild woman and somehow evading Carlos, who was caught on the other side of the fight. Dale brought his elbow up to block her assault, then jammed the edge of it into her jaw. The blow sent her head snapping backward, ending her struggle and allowing Carlos to restrain her.

He held her arms pinned behind her. Dale wiped blood from his nose. "You stupid, little bitch." He slapped her across the cheek, then shoved his face so close to hers she smelled the eggs he had had for breakfast. His face burned bright red.

"This is my ship," he screamed, spittle flying from his lips. "You do what I say."

She flinched and shook from the sudden surge of adrenaline.

"I thought your Armadan would have taught you more about obedience."

Mari mustered a defiance she didn't feel and stared at Dale. "David's not like that."

"Well, Carlos is. He won't hesitate to give you a lesson in respect."

She stared at the big man, knowing from the scowl on his face that this was no idle threat.

Carlos shoved her into a seat as though she were a child and pulled the heavy canvas restraints across her chest, smashing her breasts with his forearm. She bit her lip against the pain, not wanting to give either of the men the satisfaction of seeing her hurt and humiliated. He cinched the straps down so hard she fought for shallow breaths. Her hands fumbled at the straps.

Carlos forced them down at her sides. She kicked at him as he secured her arms with the adjoining strap. When she made contact with his groin, he grabbed her by the throat.

"Before you leave this ship," he whispered, "I'm going to hurt you in ways you never knew a man could hurt a woman."

She couldn't move—she could hardly breathe.

Carlos and Dale settled in beside her.

The surge of take-off pushed her further into her seat, making it almost impossible to draw a breath. She tried to suck air into her lungs, her heart pounding in her ears, but the restraints crushed her. She feebly tried to dislodge them with her hands. The g-force worked against her and the blackness of suffocation sparkled in front of her vision. This couldn't be happening. Her mind went blank as a freakish calm swept over her and she lost her battle with consciousness.

I lost her.

The *Thrall's* engines pitched higher and the concrete beneath David's feet vibrated. A huge shadow passed overhead as the big ship pushed away from the dock and drifted out above the ocean. It hit the launch lane in a matter of seconds. Once its main thrusters kicked in, the *Thrall 7* lifted into the cloudless blue sky. It accelerated with every kilometer, powering toward escape velocity.

"We have to get back to the *Bard*. I can catch that ship." David spun around, right into a cender planted in his chest.

"The only place you're going is a holding cell." It was the female contractor from earlier today. The icy blue of her eyes matched her tone.

"On what charges?" David asked. Had they already found out about the stolen fast track?

"An illegal docking."

"Sounds kinky," Sean said. "I don't think he's into that kind of shit."

As soon as the dark-haired woman glanced in Sean's direction, David grabbed her wrist and twisted. The cender tumbled to the concrete where Sean scrambled for it, but this contractor wasn't as green as Ward. She kicked the weapon under the cargo container and jammed the top of her head into David's jaw.

Blood swam in David's mouth. He squeezed her wrist tighter, working her bones against the tendons. Gritting her teeth against the pain, she went for her full holster. Sean got to it first. But as he drew the pistol, the contractor used David's own weight against him and spun him into Sean, knocking the two men into the metal container wall.

David lost his grip on her wrist, allowing her to curl away and land a kick to Sean's chest. Before he could recover, she smashed his hand against the ungiving cargo container to disarm him. Another contractor swung around the side.

The last thing David saw before tackling the female was Sean jamming his elbow into the male contractor's face.

The female went limp when David's weight slammed her to the concrete. He scanned the area for her second cender. All he saw was Ward running straight for him, both cenders aimed at David's head. David rolled off the female just before a pair of static bolts sizzled by. He scrambled for cover behind a pile of discarded pallets.

Sean and his opponent exchanged blows and kicks in David's periphery, but David kept his focus on Ward.

"You want to find out who the better man is, Ward? Put down those guns and face me in a fair fight," David yelled. "Or don't you have the balls?"

David hoped to goad the young man into a hand to hand engagement. A seasoned contractor would never take the bait because they'd know better than to give up a tactical advantage and their weapons. But David counted on Ward's need to prove himself to the big kids.

"Guns are holstered, Anlow. Any time you're ready."

"Not that I don't trust you, but I want to hear them hit the dock." He didn't have time for this. Mari was hurtling farther away from the planet each second he spent dicking around with these assholes. And every second it became more difficult to hold his anger in check.

Two clunks of metal on concrete prompted David into action. He flew from behind the pallets, knowing Ward could have drawn him out with only the promise of fighting fair, but David's rush to get to Mari made him chance it.

He wasn't prepared for the scene in front of him.

Sean stood over the male contractor's body. Blood trickled from the blonde hair at Sean's temple, out of one side of his nose, and down his right arm. But David was most concerned that Killian stood behind Sean, one of his cenders pointing at the mech tech's head, the other trained on David.

How could you be so stupid, Anlow?

He'd given up his advantage and broken a cardinal rule of engagement by rushing back into this fray blind. Now Killian had him right where he'd wanted him ever since they borrowed that berth space. So David was more surprised than anyone when Killian lowered his weapon, at least the one he held on David.

"Go ahead," he said. "I've been waiting to see you and Ward go at it for two days."

David exchanged looks with Sean to see if there was something he was missing. Sean's expression was guarded but he gave a little shrug.

Ward didn't need an invitation. He rushed David, slamming his shoulder into David's side and forcing him backward. But the impact hadn't knocked him down, so Ward landed a round house kick to David's chest, followed by a chop to his neck with the knife edge of his hand.

All control snapped inside David. He blocked two more quick jabs from Ward, then took the offensive.

The contractor might be younger and faster, but David was pissed. He absorbed Ward's blows not worrying about injuries, concentrating only on punishing Ward for keeping him from Mari. David held onto Ward's arm, then buried his fist in Ward's kidney.

Ward returned the favor with a knife slash across the scorched skin on David's back. *So much for fighting fair.* The pain was a good focus—David spun Ward around by his trapped arm and threw him to the ground.

Ward scrambled away and lunged for his cender, but David was right there, forcing Ward's arm above his head. The static tingled through David's body a second before a sizzling shot thudded into the cargo container, blasting hot shrapnel across the boardwalk and barely missing Sean and Killian. David jammed his thumb into the tendons of Ward's wrist. Reflexively his hand opened, dropping the cender to the concrete.

David twisted Ward's arm and brought it down hard over his raised knee. The appendage didn't snap, but Ward cried out with the pain. A flash of disbelief, then fear invaded Ward's eyes. David seized him by the throat with one hand, slamming him back to the concrete. Then David was on top of him, smashing his fist into Ward's face repeatedly.

The rumors that Armadans snapped into a crazed berserker mode when pushed too far held a bit of truth to them. That they could switch on aggressor genes was ludicrous, a dark parable the Embassy perpetuated to frighten children or to give themselves a false sense of control over their own military. The spike of adrenaline and single-minded focus David was experiencing right now had nothing to do with the switching on of genes—it was pure bloodlust.

The more of Ward's blood that splashed onto the concrete, the more of it David wanted. He was certain the bones in his fingers had fractured, but not as badly as Ward's jaw and orbital socket.

"If you don't finish him off, I'll just pretend he fell." Killian's voice barely registered.

"David." Sean spoke up. "That guy's not worth it. We have a way out of this and we need to go. For Mari."

Those last words stopped David's fist mid-swing. "Why the out, Killian?"

The contractor grinned. "Ward liked to score points with my superiors...by running his mouth. You helped me shut his mouth."

The son-of-a-bitch wanted me to do his dirty work.

David stood up. "I'm not sure Ward will remember *falling.*"

"As badly as you beat him, I'm not sure Ward will remember much of anything." Killian nudged Ward's arm with the toe of his boot. "But, I'll make sure he remembers it the right way."

"Why not finish him?" David asked.

"He's married to my half-sister, and she happens to be my favorite." Killian said the last part in a way that left nothing open for interpretation.

"What about the other two?" Sean inclined his chin toward the female and other male sprawled unconscious and bleeding on the concrete.

"I had to make it look legit," Killian said. "But I'd suggest you leave now before one of them wakes up and sees us talking all nice-like."

"How legit is it going to look if you don't have a scratch on you?" Sean asked before spinning around and clocking Killian in the jaw.

David thought he was going to see Sean get his head blown off, but Killian just rubbed his jaw and said between clenched teeth, "Guess I don't have to worry about that now."

"Let's go, Sean," David warned.

He didn't trust Killian in the least, but they were wasting time. He'd face the consequences of this run-in later he was sure, but he would take the out for now.

Killian kept a cender pointed between them as David and Sean backed around the cargo container to rejoin the main dock. Then they ran for the fast track.

We can't catch a break.

"I guess we should have expected someone to notice a missing fast track," David said.

They stared at the empty section of waterfront where they had made their impromptu docking. Nothing but the lapping remnants of a distant ferry's wake. Every second they lost bouncing around here at Shiraz ripped Mari farther away from him.

"We'll have trouble following the *Thrall* on our own at this rate," Sean said. "The *Bard* is faster than a freighter any day, but we're playing catch up now. We need help, specifically their flight plan."

"On it." David sent a transmission to his brother as they headed toward the industrial docks exit. Thankfully, security wasn't as tight leaving the area.

His reporter buzzed and a screen opened across his palm. A pretty female trooper, her blonde hair twisted into an elegant braid crowning her head, responded to David's call.

"Captain Anlow." She saluted. *"Petty Officer First Class Alexa Collins, sir."*

Habit almost had him saluting back. He didn't recognize the young woman, but he'd been in command of an entire warship just last year, so thousands of troopers knew his face. Talk about another lifetime.

"Petty Officer Collins, is Lieutenant Anlow available? This is an emergency."

"Your brother's on bunk time, but I'll notify him immediately to report for your call to the nearest communications port."

"Thank you."

"May I just say quickly, sir, that it was an honor to serve under you on the Protector *last year."*

A lump caught in David's throat. He couldn't fall into the regret of nostalgia right now. Not with Mari's life on the line.

"Thank you, Petty Officer," was all he said before ending the transmission.

"We're drawing our share of attention," Sean said.

Passersby gave David and Sean a wide berth. Both men were dirty and bruised. Sean had blood trickling down his arm and part of his face, and a scorch mark blazed across David's back.

"I hope we can get out of here without running into any guards," David said.

"Or more contractors."

Mari didn't have time for them to be questioned.

"I have an idea." Sean veered toward the roadway abutting the berths. Before David could ask him what the hell he was thinking Ben's return call came through. David didn't wait for him to say hello.

"I need you to track a freighter called *Thrall 7*. Dale Zapona has Mari on that ship. It just left berth six-two-four from Shiraz."

Ben repeated the request to Petty Officer Collins. If Ben were bunking this close to the command center onboard ship, it meant he was either in the process of a multiple-day briefing or debriefing. When David was a junior officer, he hated the latter more—higher ups calling you in for questioning at all hours, ripping you from sleep to confirm or deny some ridiculous detail. Then he became a ship's captain and found it was indeed necessary to put his officers and troopers through the same exercise, just like he was doing to poor Ben. Except David couldn't remember a more dire situation.

"We're requesting their flight plan. As soon as I get it, I'll transmit it to you. I'm going to match it against their route, too, just in case it's bogus." Redness rimmed Ben's eyes, but he never gave an indication of being bothered. Not so much as a yawn. He was a good soldier, a good brother, and probably David's best friend.

"Thanks."

"What else can I do?"

Sean suddenly zipped out in front of a transport heading their way. David thought for sure Sean would be run over, but the driver squealed to a halt so close to him, Sean pounded on the hood before running to confront the man inside.

"Nothing. Unless you can send a gunship after them." David almost wished Ben had that kind of power, but that would be abuse of authority. Then Ben would be in as much trouble as David was right now.

"You know I would if I could."

The transport driver shouted as Sean manhandled him out of his seat.

"I have to go, Ben. I'll be waiting for that flight plan."

David joined Sean at the transport, shoving the ousted driver aside and jumping into the passenger seat.

Mari opened her mouth to scream, but water rushed in. She inhaled and choked. Her hands batted around her in a panic as she forced her eyes open against the pressure of the blurring liquid.

Calloused hands jostled her out from under the running water.

"David?"

She searched for his face, but stared at a man she didn't recognize...at first.

"Did you forget about me already?" Carlos's voice brought all the horrifying reality of the day rushing back at her.

"Where are we?" She glanced around to get her bearings. From the rancid smell, she thought it might be a bathroom or a filthy, mildewed shower stall, but there were no walls separating this part of the five meter square room from the rest of it. Carlos turned the water off from a spigot sticking out of a ceramic tile wall halfway up. The drain just below it swallowed the liquid slowly, belching some of it back. She gagged as it brought the putrid smell up into the room.

Carlos dragged her by one arm across the tile floor back onto a rubberized base like that in the commonway. The unforgiving surface chafed against her bare legs. But that pain seemed small compared to how her jaw throbbed. And her teeth felt loose. When she attempted deeper breaths, her chest burned, so she stuck to shallow breathing—it helped with the smell in any event.

A bunk with rumpled bedding was fastened to one wall while a single metal chair sat in the opposite corner.

"Do I have to chain you to that wall the whole way to Sinder Isle or are you going to do what you're told?" Carlos loomed over her.

She lowered her gaze, not wanting to look at him. "I'll do what I'm told." She was too exhausted to do much of anything. Besides, she would have no chance of escape if she were shackled inside this room.

"That's a good girl," he said.

She didn't like the insinuation in his tone.

"Stand up."

She pushed off the floor and tried her shaky legs, but still avoided his scrutinizing stare. She wrapped her arms around herself, and not just to ward off the sudden chill of being soaked.

Carlos moved toward her. He pushed her chin up to study her face. "Are those freaky eyes the first thing you see when you look in the mirror? Chairman Zapona thinks that means your genes are worthless. You're no better than Lower Caste trash as far as he's concerned."

She twisted away from Carlos. The insult stung her like a slap across the face.

He reached to touch her again, but she backed away from him.

Carlos snorted. "You don't have to be shy. Your fucked up genes don't bother me. I've docked my share of Lowers. They bend over and take it just like any other woman."

"I'm not a Lower."

Mari attempted to put more space between them, but realized he had backed her against the wall. Placing his hands against the space on either side of her, he penned her in. She turned her head to the side because she felt smothered by his chest.

He leaned down and whispered against her neck, sending waves of nausea and fear through her stomach. "You know, if you're into Armadans, one is just as good as another." He pressed so close to her she could feel his erection through his pants. "It'll make the trip go faster. I won't be as rough as Stavros will be, but I do owe you for that kick to the balls you gave me at launch."

Carlos jammed his hips into hers, smashing her pelvis against the wall painfully. She tried to wedge her arms between them to push him off, but couldn't move.

"You're just a tiny thing, young too. I bet your pilot likes that. Means you're tight."

Mari shook, but finally looked at Carlos with what she hoped was overwhelming defiance. "You don't know anything about him."

"He was a fleet officer. Even if I hadn't read his official record, his arrogant bearing would have given him away. I hated the officers when I was in the Armada, always taking away my privileges for one infraction or another. It's going to feel good to take something from one of them." Carlos sucked on her neck.

"Get away from me." She tried to shove him again, but he snatched her upper arms in an iron grip, then grabbed one of her breasts so tightly it brought tears to her eyes.

She spit in his face.

He wiped the mess off with the back of his hand slowly, then in a lightning fast motion grabbed her by the hair and pulled tight, jerking her neck painfully to the side.

"I like your fight," Carlos said. "But save it for Stavros. You'll need it with that psychopath because no matter what I do to you, he'll do worse."

"That may be." Dale's voice bounced around in the sparse room. *"But he'll also want our little blonde as pristine as possible upon delivery. Why else do you think he wants them so young? As much debt as you have, Carlos, I'm sure you won't want to ruin a payday like last time. She's not worth it. Find a Lower at a flesh club who looks like her, then play out your revenge fantasies."*

It took a moment, but Carlos finally pushed away from the wall.

Now that she had a little space, Mari felt bolder. "Is this what you planned last year when you hired me on Deleine?" She searched the ceiling until she spotted a camera in one corner. She walked over to stand just below it, knowing Dale was looking down on her.

"Why else would I bother with you?" His voice now crackled from behind her.

She noticed the speakers set into the ceiling.

"Ironically, the only thing of value you have to offer me is your genetic pollution. Because let's face it. You're not much of a scientist."

Carlos chuckled.

"Now settle in. We'll be there before you know it."

Mari watched Carlos until the door slid closed behind him. Tears rolled down her cheeks so she kept her back to the camera. Dale wouldn't have the satisfaction. She surveyed the steel walls of her temporary prison and suddenly became paralyzed by her fear and humiliation. How did her world morph into this nightmare so fast? This morning she had woken up in David's arms, feeling like she could conquer the world, get her career back on track, live the life she had planned. Her conscious mind barely accepted this sudden reversal.

Probably because acceptance would mean the end for her.

I'm going to kill you in a hundred different ways.

As David prepared the *Bard* for takeoff, he imagined all of Dale Zapona's deaths—each one slower and messier than the last one.

The black torbernite floor of the bridge threatened to swallow David, just like the darkness of his mood. Maybe because it felt as though the gun metal grey walls pressed a little closer with each ticking minute. Even the late afternoon sun glittering on the bay out of the cockpit window mocked him, reminding him he couldn't freeze time for Mari. Or reverse it, taking them back to this morning, wrapped in the colorful cheer of her room. He'd tell her to forget about her meeting with Dale, convince her to stay in bed all day, delighting in their new closeness.

David blamed himself as much for Mari's abduction as he did Dale. The guilt and helplessness of waiting slashed away the calm David had barely regained after his encounter with the contractors. For the first time in decades, David had succumbed to bloodlust. Ward was the hapless, though not innocent, victim. Throughout David's service in the fleet, he'd seen bloodlust many times in some of his troopers, and he had only a few times experienced that blinding aggression to which Armadans were genetically prone. The sensation still echoed through his veins.

As he waited for clearance to leave, he stared at the vid of Mari and him kissing on Shiraz Dock. Ben had sent it in the guise of a joke yesterday, but David knew his brother was actually sentimental and figured David would want to keep the memory. Ben was right. David had come to cherish this little clip of his life since Dale had taken Mari from him.

Maybe David should have gone to the authorities, but he had no real proof that Mari was even with the man. Perhaps Ben had found out something else in this last half hour. But then he would have contacted David immediately with any news. It was wishful thinking…and wishes were for children.

I will bring you home, Mari.

Funny how, not two days ago, David hadn't accepted the *Bard* as home, but now that he associated the ship with Mari it felt like *theirs.*

Footsteps sounded in the commonway leading to the bridge. David closed the air screen.

"I have their flight plan." Sean stepped inside and walked through the emptiness where Mari and David's image had been a second before.

How Sean managed to obtain the *Thrall*'s flight plan before Ben's fleet connections would be a topic for conversation later. Right now David was just grateful for the information.

Solimar Robbins entered behind Sean and strapped into the crash couch on the far wall of the bridge. Normally she stayed in her suite during takeoff and landing because of her *sensitivity* to g-forces. David hoped she was here now out of concern for Mari and not so she would have a first-hand account of whatever happened for her archives.

"Feed me the coordinates." David prompted the holo-controls. A glowing, transparent orb enveloped the pilot's chair.

Sean had already called up the co-pilot's seat and its controls. The simmering anger David held in check heated to a boil. Not because it was Sean sitting in the chair beside David, but because it *wasn't* Mari.

"I uploaded the projected route and where they should be along it at this point," Sean said. "We might not be able to intercept them before they reach Deleine."

"You said the *Bard* could catch a freighter any day," David snapped. A lot could happen to Mari on the *Thrall* during that time, none of which he was prepared to face.

Sean's tone was even and a little quiet. "On the short run we could because we have speed in the beginning, but the freighter picks up its pace exponentially the farther it goes. We max out."

"Even if you add another cylinder to our reactor?"

"I already have. It's loaded and ready to kick in once we clear atmosphere, but we'd be lucky to catch them before they land. Maybe a few hours afterward, but…."

David stared at his controls. "You're sure?"

"Yeah. In fact, I was being generous with the odds. It doesn't make me feel too good either."

"I can't believe this is happening," Solimar said barely above a whisper.

Neither can I.

The comm sounded with a go ahead for lift-off from Shiraz. David wouldn't give up while there was still a chance. And maybe Ben could come through with some unauthorized fleet help after all.

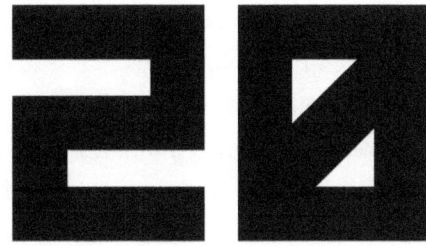

"Stop watching me!"

Mari stared at the corner camera. The little green light below its lens stared back at her. She was sure that behind that lens Dale, or worse, Carlos, was observing everything she did in this little prison cell.

"Someone's going to come for me. And you're both going to be convicted of abduction. That carries a big sentence."

At least she assumed it did. The Media never reported much on abductions, either because there weren't many or she just never heard about them on the channels she watched. The glitz of fashion and celebrities didn't mix well with the suffering of real people. A small part of her always felt a kinship to the wealthy, carefree celebrities. She thought by leaving Deleine she could have a similar life. That dream soon evaporated, and her circumstances right now left no doubt that she was, and maybe always had been by consequence of birth, one of the people meant to suffer.

Mari picked up the chair and lobbed it at the protruding surveillance box. Her feeble attempt fell short of its mark. She picked it up again and stood closer. This time it caught the bottom of the grey plastic box and dislodged the camera inside. The less delicate camera, encased in metal and no bigger than her fist, hit the rubber floor, but bounced and rolled without much real damage. She lifted the chair and smashed the camera's housing over and over, pretending it was Carlos's head. Or Dale's. She hated them both.

'The only thing of value you have to offer is your genetic pollution.' Dale's words from earlier still taunted her.

Though Mari had always been self-conscious about her eyes, she had never thought of their uniqueness as an indicator for faulty genes. Only certain families had these particular genetic markers which left them susceptible to the reaction she had had from her childhood vaccines. It was rare. She was the only one out of all of her brothers, sisters, and cousins—one hundred seventy total in that particular generation—whose irises faded and distorted from their deep, rich brown to a pale coral.

Finding out why Mari had the reaction when no one else in her family did was what prompted her to study medicine in the first place. She had a secret desire that she barely admitted to herself—she always thought she could find a way to reverse the pigment change.

Though the doctors from her town, including her uncle, assured her there was nothing wrong with her, that the effect was a random mutation, Mari believed there *was* something wrong with her, a sentiment that others casually, at times knowingly, reinforced with their stares, their cruel comments, their avoidance.

David had never avoided her. In fact, he went out of his way to engage her. She put the chair down lightly as she thought about how he looked into her distinctive eyes as though enchanted, especially while they coupled. He was gentle and giving even though his body was hard and strong. She had never met a man like him, couldn't imagine any others even existed. Now she might not see him again. She might not see anyone again.

A sob almost burst from her throat. The next man to touch her so intimately would not be David, would not be so kind, would—according to Dale—want to see tears drowning her coral-colored irises from pain. All because she was different. She never hated what the reaction had done to her more than at this moment.

She heaved the chair above her head again with tired arms when she noticed the camera's battery chamber lay exposed through a crack in the metal. As she tossed the chair aside, an idea was already forming. The first spark of hope since her abduction.

Settling cross-legged on the dirty rubber flooring, she snatched up the damaged camera to inspect it further. She tried prying the casing open, but managed only to bloody the pads of her fingers. The battery remained snug in its chamber, teasing her. She wiped her hands on her white shirt, the stains blending with the filth already ground into the fabric. There had to be something in this sparse cell she could use for a tool. The chair seemed impervious to all manner of abuse, considering she'd barely dented the frame after her attack on the camera housing. A drip from behind her drew her attention to the disgusting spigot area.

The handle.

She abandoned the camera and scampered onto the wet tile in her bare feet. The puddled water squished between her toes, its chill sending a splinter of cold through her whole body. She reached for the handle and twisted it. Water gurgled out and slapped onto the tile. She kept twisting and felt a slight give. Using both hands on the oblong piece of solid metal, she forced one turn of the handle, breaking it off at a weak spot. Mari sprinted back to the camera, not caring about the water free-flowing into the backed up drain.

The handle was about the same size as her middle finger, but the torque it exerted against the casing did what her flesh couldn't. The crack expanded. Holding the camera steady with one hand, she fished her little finger into the space. Her nail caught on the edge of the battery, which was only as big as the pad of her thumb. Mari held her breath to keep steady as she maneuvered the battery toward the opening. Just as she got the battery halfway out, it slipped off her finger and tumbled back inside.

"Shit."

She tamped down her frustration and tried again. This time she twisted her finger just enough to avoid the same circumstance as her first attempt. When she extracted the battery and held its feathery weight in her hand, she laughed out loud. This little thing was going to save her life. She hoped.

"No, it will work." She spoke the words out loud as an affirmation. "It'll work."

Carlos waited in Dale's lounge for him to react to the camera going offline after the blonde had beaten it right off the wall. He was actually surprised she had it in her. Her unexpected fight stirred his arousal again.

Dale only glanced at the dark screen labeled *CELL 4* among the silver-framed monitors on the cobalt-colored wall to their left. He said nothing as he sipped one of those stupid fruity neons. The florescent colors were off-putting enough, but the mango smell of the ultra-sweet drink completely eclipsed any trace of alcohol. It made Carlos want to hold Dale's mouth open as he poured a fifth of bourbon down his gullet just so he could feel a man's drink burn down his throat and into his gut.

His boss turned his attention back to the five Media screens against the far wall of his suite's lounge. This was how Dale spent most of his time during flights on his freighters—holed up in a luxury suite, which cost as much to overhaul as it would to refurbish the entire crew level. He cycled through the various feeds until he found a sex vid for the huge main screen and twenty-five hour news and celebrity feeds from all six planet moons to fill up the smaller screens flanking the middle one.

He turned down the grunting and moaning and upped the volume on an animated debate among the Quorum of Archivists, which played out on the bottom corner screen.

"I'm just saying that someone needs to do something about these fraggers before they get organized." Archivist Andravo made the point to a smattering of applause from some of the other delegates.

"That's just it. They aren't organized, simply a hodge-podge of disenfranchised Lower Caste activists who happen to be a little tech savvy. Hardly anything to call in the Armada for...." Phoebe Llewellyn, now that was a woman who could make even an apathetic man give a shit about politics. She had a knockout body and that blue streaked hair did something for Carlos.

But hearing her prattle on had him losing interest fast, especially as the porn vid switched to an up-close shot of a blonde woman performing fellatio on a man tied to a chair. The image fed Carlos's carnal appetite. He imagined—*what's her name? Maria? Mari? Yeah, Mari, that was it.* He imagined forcing Mari to her knees to act out this same scene. Only he sure as shit wasn't going to let her tie him to a chair.

"I'll go straighten things out in that cell," Carlos said, rapping on the blank monitor with his knuckles.

If Dale wasn't going to give him the order, he'd be happy to volunteer to handle this situation in his own way. No camera, no mic, no way for Dale to see Carlos having a little fun. He could take his time with her. Then he'd dose her so she wouldn't rat him out. He'd explain that he thought it would be easier to hand her over that way, and they'd be gone before Dale knew he had damaged Stavros's merchandise...again.

"Don't bother." Dale stopped Carlos in his tracks. "So what if she destroyed the camera. She's not getting out of that cell unless we open the door for her."

Perturbed, Carlos pushed the issue. "And if she hurts herself? Will Stavros still pay?"

Dale paused the Media screen where news about the Embassy's new Ambasadora project had been breaking.

"Point taken. Guess that's why you're the security guy." Dale's tone hinted at derision. "Check on her. Put her in another cell if you have to."

"I'll take care of her," Carlos said. This trip was proving to be one of the better ones.

About time.

David put Ben's transmission through on the bridge. "Tell me you found them."

"Yeah, closer than expected. The freighter looks to be heading toward Tampa Deux's orbit, not Deleine like their official route says."

"Which dock on Tampa Deux?"

"Don't know that yet. We probably won't know until just before they land. I have my team keeping tabs on the chatter from the larger docks, but there are thousands of smaller municipal docks that we don't have the resources to cover. And, if you throw in the private ones, well, we might not know until the last minute where they're going to touch down, even with eyes on them non-stop."

David's hope gave way to this newest concern. They would be able to catch the *Thrall* now, but once Dale made it on-planet with Mari, he could make her disappear and there would be no evidence that she was ever even with him.

"I'm adjusting course toward Tampa Deux," David said. "Keep feeding me the *Thrall's* coordinates. As soon as you get an LZ for them, contact the local contractors' guild. But...." David glanced at Sean. "Best to leave my name out of this. I had another run-in with Killian and his group. It ended pretty badly."

"Understood." Ben's voice betrayed nothing, but the little pause said volumes. *"Are you going to need some help with that?"*

"Not sure there's much you'll be able to do for me there." Especially if Ward's need for vengeance trumped whatever dirt Killian had on the young man. But David would worry about that once he made sure Mari was safe.

"I'll be in touch. Until then, I've sent the latest coordinates and a couple of projected routes."

"Thanks." David ended the transmission.

"What do you mean by another run-in, David?" Soli's voice relayed her concern.

He felt badly for having assumed she was interested in this incident only for the gossip it would feed.

"Nothing to worry about," Sean spoke up. "It will blow over."

"Since when did you become the optimist?" David asked.

"Since things got this bad."

That's what I figured.

"Get me out of here." Mari channeled all her pent up fear and frustration into a battle cry. "Get. Me. Out."

She pounded on the door as she screamed. That's how she had spent the last fifteen minutes, and her vocal cords could hold out a lot longer than that.

Boots clomped on the other side of the door. She fell silent in anticipation, listening to the gush of water still streaming out of the broken spigot and inundating the tile floor. She grabbed the chair and held it up so she could swing it like a club. Her body was so tense, her muscles felt like they could snap her bones if this lasted any longer.

The door slid open.

Mari swung the chair, twisting her body with the effort.

The chair crashed along the side of Carlos's shoulder and head. But the cast metal frame didn't appear to do more than knock him off balance and draw a blossoming crimson stain in his cropped blonde hair.

He stumbled away from her, grabbing his head. "I'm going to cut you open myself."

Mari glanced down to be sure she hadn't strayed from the rubber flooring, then flicked the little battery at Carlos's feet…right into the pooling water. The battery exploded as soon as it hit the liquid, unleashing electrical arcs into Carlos. His body convulsed from the current. Those compact batteries might be small, but like Mari, they held a lot of energy.

Mari jumped through the cell door, slamming it closed before running down the commonway.

"Okay, next step."

She chattered to herself as she criss-crossed the commonways, searching for the hydroponics lab, not caring that the slapping of her bare feet on the rubber floor sounded like the cadence of Armadan troopers.

"Where is it?" She chanced a peek at the ceiling, not quite able to see into the darkness above with only the runner lights on the floor for illumination. Was that another surveillance box? She couldn't be sure, but thought she'd also seen one in the previous commonway. If so, all the cameras out here were up and functioning so Dale could track her movements with ease.

She wandered from one long commonway into another, looking for a conduit and vents.

"There." A nest of tubes snaking along the wall and ceiling.

The thick blue hose vented excess carbon dioxide into space, the green banded tube carried liquid fertilizer through the ship's refuse system to be recycled. The yellow banded tube carried sugars—monosaccharides and polysaccharides—to the kitchen. Mari just needed to figure out in which direction the liquid was flowing. She ran, watching the tube until she felt heat increasing.

"Wrong way." She'd only run into oven exhaust if she kept in this direction, so she backtracked and followed the little yellow bands the other way. Soon this tube was joined by a small grey and white banded tube—liquid condensate from the ship's respiratory system. This was the very water the plants in the hydroponics bay needed to survive.

The next left rewarded her with the subtle sound of a humming condenser and lengths of chubby orange filtration pipes running along the wall. Their familiar structures were her guide. She picked up her pace, already winded, but determined.

As soon as she hit the door to the hydroponics bay, she pulled out the spigot handle she'd tucked inside her bra. Hopefully it was stronger than the metal cover hiding the control panel for the lock. And just thin enough to jam under the cover as a lever. It was a tight fit and the smooth, rounded edges of the handle kept slipping off the cover as she tried to use the piece as a mini pry bar.

"Concentrate!"

She took a deep breath and began once more, willing herself not to look over her shoulder. If they caught her this time, it was over. She manipulated the handle under a corner of the cover. Not giving up any ground, but being careful not to let the little metal handle slip again. It had become the greatest multi-tool the system had ever seen. She wiggled the handle back and forth. Centimeter by centimeter she worked it under the cover. This was taking longer than she expected.

Pop.

The seal broke. She let the cover fall away and studied the blue glowing wires in front of her. Relief passed through her to see the wiring was standard, just like on the *Bard*. She searched her mind, trying to remember how Sean had hot-wired the *Bard*'s bridge door when their old pilot had passed out at the controls and *accidentally* changed the lock codes. That had only been six weeks ago. She should be able to remember Sean's steps exactly. She certainly remembered him beating the piss out of the pilot once he got inside.

Closing her eyes, she recalled Sean's nimble fingers flying through the steps. She'd always taken her photographic memory and knack for mnemonic devices for granted—the only thing they seemed to be good for was school—but they might actually save her. Mari touched a rainbow of plastic insulators at the nexus of the wires, finally choosing the red one. Red she had associated with clay, no good for growing plants. And this wire was no good for opening doors.

Next. Orange. Like her eyes. An unexpected outcome. Avoid the orange insulator. She moved onto yellow, but couldn't remember there being a yellow insulator in the *Bard*'s panel. Or was there? In her panic to recreate the memory, the images started coming to her too quickly. Forcing her memory to slow down, Mari worked each step as Sean had, removing insulators and crimping some of the remaining wires, regardless of color. She re-clamped each insulator back to its wire at the crimp and watched the blue glow blink out. It was like cutting off the circulation to a limb with a tourniquet.

When she removed the black insulator, the wire beneath it flashed green. That hadn't happened with any of the other wires.

"And that didn't happen to Sean."

Or maybe he had severed the wire's connection before it could flash a warning. What's the worst that could happen if she did that now? A shipload of electricity would fry her where she stood. Thinking about being tortured to death and having her eyes cut out made the risk of electrocution worth it. Using the plastic insulator, she crimped the wire and secured it.

The door hissed open. She leaped inside and punched the emergency lock by the door frame to seal her in the hydroponics bay. Someone with enough tech knowledge or brute force would probably be able to break in, but that would take a while.

She took a breath. Organic smells, reminiscent of wet leaves on concrete, floated on the humidity inside the huge bay. Unlike the rest of the ship, bright lights shined from the ceiling, blasting the plants with UV rays. This artificial sunlight gave her hope, an oasis from the dreary commonways and her cell. She had always taken refuge in plants and flowers when her spirits were low back on Deleine, but this was taking it to a whole new level.

The area must have covered a space that was twenty times the size of that pitiful cell they'd locked her in. She moved among the beautiful bounty—tomato *trees*, their vines trussed to form a canopy where perfect red fruit hung underneath, their smell not quite as robust as those that came from the soil back home. But the dwarf orange and lemon trees forming the other side of this space orchard scented the air with their citrus aroma. This was how she remembered her scentbots smelling, when she could still catch a whiff of their fragrance from her skin.

Rows of soy beans and high-yielding wheat sprouted from a sea of brilliant white containers at the end of the tree-lined tunnel. In the next section white pillars as broad as David's chest reached from floor to ceiling. Feathery leaf lettuce and greens in several varieties dotted the pillars' smooth surfaces. Several hanging gardens with exposed roots brushed against Mari's arm as she admired their bounty of edible and fruit-producing plants in vivid reds and purples.

An oasis of dwarf palms, heavy with dates, rounded out one end of the bay, reminding Mari of Dale's conservatory, but too clean, too sterile. The only hint of imperfection was an array of white storage and mixing containers strewn along the wall behind the brown, shedding trunks, as though someone had been working with them then found something better to do.

The foliage crammed into this impressive space represented years of genetic science and research, tweaking and modification of hundreds of thousands, if not millions, of species.

Resentment at Dale's earlier comment about Mari's genetic pollution burned at her. Society had no problem manipulating the genes of vegetation, but had lawful taboos about enhancing or changing animals and humans. Yet it was this same science, honed and fostered on the worldships so long ago, which aided in the beautification of the Upper Caste in the first place. Selective breeding was still gene manipulation no matter if you covered it with the euphemism of marriage.

"And defects are still defects."

As if in response to her voice breaking the silence, the aeration system kicked on, spraying its automatic mist of nutrient-rich water over the roots and scaring her out of her skin. A good reminder that she wasn't out of danger. For her plan to succeed, she needed to get to the bridge. In order for that to happen, she needed a big distraction—nothing was bigger than venting part of the ship.

The layout of this bay should be rudimentary, yet the condensers weren't where she expected them to be. The only other place left was the area near the nutrient mixers, beyond a copse of dwarf evergreen and deciduous trees. But even someone with her limited experience in hydroponics design knew that placing the condensers too close to the mixers was a bad idea. They both ran hot and one could cause the other to overheat. This was either a poor design or a tactic to cut costs. Either way it made Mari's job easier.

A purple glow emanating from the angled lower branches of an avocado tree caught her attention. The dim light came from some hot pink and white bromeliads clumped in the fork of the small tree. She'd only seen this species of bromeliad in vids from her botany classes. They were extremely rare, found only in the embargoed Archenzon rain forest on Tampa One. These were most likely contraband. It didn't surprise Mari that Dale was into cultivating illegal plants—that infringement paled in comparison to human trafficking.

The aerators kicked off, leaving behind the tinkling drips from exposed roots as the left-over liquid was funneled into a reclamation filter. The sound helped to soothe her as she surveyed the bank of condensers and mixers.

She accessed the sensors for the air filtration system, which was hooked directly into the condensers.

All she had to do was crank up the oxygen, then override the vacuum sensor, allowing the vents to unseal. They were made for keeping the CO_2 levels balanced. She calculated in her head what percentage would make this system go critical. It wasn't a uniform amount. It all depended upon the size of the space, what kind and how many plants and trees were contained within the bay, and how strong the CO_2 scrubbers were.

The easiest and fastest way to emergency ventilate *on-planet* was by opening the vents to the outside. It was never supposed to happen in space due to the catastrophic consequences, but the sensors were ridiculously easy to override.

With the vacuum of empty, endless space on the other side of that wall, one little broken seal was all she needed—that would be enough to start the venting process and draw all attention to the hydroponics bay. Of course, she needed to get out of the bay first before the compartment barricade came crashing down to keep the rest of the ship safe from this damaged section. She also needed to do all this without running into anyone.

She worked frantically on the vent override, opting to do it manually by disrupting the vacuum signal instead of wasting time with codes. Sean was the code master—Mari only knew the physical components from the design. The previous botanist cheated Dale by skipping redundancy measures and using cheap parts.

Though the vent controls were one of the most important features of any hydroponics bay, it was the one which failed most often, due to lack of attention to detail. Designers, techs, and laborers who worked cheap and fast were usually to blame for greenshift failures.

When she finally wiggled the vacuum sensor out of its nest of wires, she expected to be compensated with alarms and flashing emergency lights, but nothing changed. The oxygen hadn't reached critical levels yet. Good. She needed the extra time to get out.

A metal panel slid up on the entry door back to her left, revealing a window looking out into the commonway. Mari scampered behind a series of staked cacao plants.

She could make out Carlos's blood-streaked scalp just outside. His head was bent down as he, no doubt, worked to rewire her lockout. He must have triggered the window shade by accident. She needed to figure out how to evade Carlos once he made it through that door. Hopefully he hadn't seen her yet.

She watched an O2 meter. By her calculations, once it hit 30%, it would open and begin to vent. Right now it lingered at 25.5%. She adjusted one of the CO2 scrubbers.

25.75%.

26%.

It climbed faster now.

26.5%.

Maybe too fast.

She crawled back into the rows of herbs so she could have a clear shot for the door as soon as Carlos popped inside. If he couldn't get the door open, she'd have to open it from this side and try to charge past him, otherwise she'd start to feel the effects of hypoxia and hyperventilate. Then she'd die. Right before she got sucked out into space. Or at least she hoped it would be in that order.

She felt a little light-headed. A bleating alarm made her whole body jump. The oxygen had just gone critical. She had to get out…now.

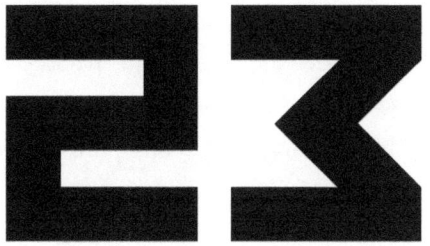

They were so close, and that's what made waiting unbearable.

David stared into space, following the faint light of a craft passing tens of thousands of miles away from them and heading into the atmosphere of Tampa Deux. He was even farther away from Mari at this point and the thought burned into his brain. He felt powerless.

David had never been good at relinquishing power without a fight, and that wasn't always a good thing. They'd tried to beat it out of him in the fleet with the lash, but that only worked to make him shrewder in the way he vied to keep control, not just of his emotions, but of the state of affairs. With forty-five years of experience as a soldier and most of those as an officer, he had learned how to finesse control, giving a little when he could, taking it forcefully when necessary, like when Lyra had mutinied on the *Argo Protector.*

'This isn't personal, Captain Anlow.'

That was the comment which had made him snap. It summed up how Lyra viewed their entire relationship—cold, impersonal, lost among titles and positions. It had also been the fuel he needed to physically wrestle control away from her, ending her mutiny with a swift reversal of a cender. Then he left her and her cohorts on a salt plain in an underpopulated area of Tampa One to wait for the prison ship.

She'd accused him of abandoning them to die, but mutineers were never allowed to stay on-ship just in case they had allies still willing to take up the cause. David had followed protocol to the letter only because he wanted to see Lyra suffer. Part of him regretted it now, but what was done was done.

At least he had been able to act. *This* situation was like nothing he'd experienced before. Sitting in a nav chair on a defunct pleasure cruiser while the woman he cared about suffered any number of horrors was almost enough to put him over the edge. That had been apparent in the incident with Ward.

"We should catch up to them in about ninety minutes," Sean said.

"Ninety minutes is a long time," David said.

Sean didn't say anything.

The mood plummeted further into its own somberness.

Soli spoke up. "Mari's tougher than either of you believe. Don't let the clothes and verbosity fool you. She's got a good brain and more determination than anyone I've ever met. So don't make this sound like it's the end." Soli's voice broke.

"You're right," Sean said. "If this were Kenon we were trying to rescue, they'd have already given him back because of all the whining."

David looked at Sean. "Would we have really tried to rescue Kenon?"

Before Sean could offer a comment, the transmitter beeped with an incoming message from Ben.

"Go ahead," David said.

"If they stay on this same trajectory." Ben paused as if to emphasize that was a big if. *"We have it narrowed down to a dozen or so public docks that handle a ship that size. Should they use a ship-to-land transport, that dozen multiplies tenfold."*

"Can you intercept them before they break atmosphere?" David already knew the answer, but needed to ask.

"Not without due cause. And, unfortunately—"

"I got it," David said, knowing his word or Sean's or even Soli's wasn't enough in the face of evidence that Dale and Mari had never met this morning.

"Sorry, bro. I'll be in touch as they get closer to their destination."

David wanted to reassure Ben, but that sounded too much like giving up, and Soli's little speech from earlier had managed to inspire a faint amount of hope. David would guard that hope for Mari.

Carlos rushed into the hydroponics bay and stood in the entry, disoriented by the deafening alarm. He scanned the area.

Mari kept her head down, but circled around and peeked through the leaves of a cacao tree. She tensed her muscles, ready to bolt for the open door.

Carlos honed in on his target and charged.

Mari ran for the door as Carlos headed in the opposite direction for the open panel on the condenser housing. She hoped he'd be too concerned with the sabotage to notice her fleeing. Once at the door, she hit the emergency lock from the inside on her way out so it would seal behind her. When she saw the butchered controls on the outside, she realized that Carlos wouldn't be able to unseal the door again.

The alarm screamed through the commonway. Mari chanced a look back through the window. Carlos snapped off a length of pipe from the nutrient feeder and smashed it against the window repeatedly, barely scratching its high tension plastic surface.

His face showed signs of bloating and splotchiness as hypoxia set in, but that would be the least of his worries soon. A crash wall came snapping down in front of the door just as Carlos's body flew back toward the vents. She couldn't hear him over the alarms, but she imagined him screaming as the vacuum of space sucked him inside out trying to void the small vent holes.

She nearly vomited at the thought.

Feet pounding toward her shoved Carlos's horrific death to the back of her mind. She could consider what she'd done later. Right now she needed to get to the bridge.

She followed the pipes from earlier around the corner opposite the approaching crew and felt the increasing heat from oven exhaust. Thumbing open the first door she came to, she expected to enter the kitchen. Only the scant emergency lighting showed her this was the mess hall. She ignored the piles of dishes and silverware and focused on the two things she could use, both mounted to the corrugated metal wall. The portable fire extinguisher came out of its bracket easily enough, but she had to use it to free the map outlining fire exits and escape pod routes from its plastic frame.

According to the layout, the *Thrall*'s bridge was on this level, and at the very end of this commonway. It was a long stretch without any hiding spots. She stuffed the map into her bra, held the extinguisher to her chest, peeked out the door, and ran.

Footfalls and murmurs reached her ears from a juncture with another commonway up ahead. She readied the fire extinguisher to use as a weapon and approached the juncture with cautious steps. The rattling of silverware slapping onto the mess hall floor behind her stopped her in her tracks. She jammed her back against the wall. With her attention pulled in two directions, she suddenly felt paralyzed. Her heart raced and her palms started to sweat. Realizing she was slipping into a panic, she forced herself off the wall and sprinted past the juncture.

When no hands reached out to snag her off her feet, she felt a bit triumphant and kept moving down the long commonway. The overhead lights strobed with her pace, emphasizing the coldness of the ship within the constant play of sallow light and its infinite shadows. By the time she reached the bridge door, she was working on automatic.

"Get this right," she whispered to herself.

She slid her thumb over the door sensor. If the nav leader inside didn't respond, she'd have to hot-wire this lock, too. That could eat up time she didn't have to spare. She was about to put the fire extinguisher on the floor when the door slid open. Her surprise matched the nav leader's as they looked at one another through the entryway. Then she pounced, beaning the man over the head with the extinguisher.

Mari pulled the unconscious pilot into the commonway and scampered over him and onto the bridge, locking him out and destroying the controls to keep anyone who might be following her at bay. Though the *Thrall 7* was huge compared to the *Bard*, the bridge was practically the same size. The floor wasn't the rich black torbernite that bedecked the pleasure cruiser, however, just more of the same charcoal colored rubber. And there was no crash couch, only several wall units for about five members of the crew to use if it came down to it.

Since she planned to take over this ship, it *would* come down to it, but she'd be the only one in here. Two nav chairs waited in front of a wrap-around viewscreen that put the *Bard*'s small cockpit window to shame. She chose one of the chairs and called up an orb of holo-controls before she had even finished strapping in. The fraying fabric of the chair stank of sweat and body odor, not like the clean scent of the *Bard*'s plush leather and the leftover hint of David's green tea smell.

As soon as she put communications online, she punched in a code to transmit to the *Bard*. A message scrawled through a section of the holo-controls telling her that video messaging was unavailable. She didn't have time to fix that little bug right now.

"This is *Thrall 7* calling *Bard*." Though she didn't feel calm, she forced a slow clarity into her voice. "David. Sean. Please, someone, tell me you're listening."

Another transmission signal cut through the silence on the bridge. David opened the comm link, hoping Ben had narrowed down their variables.

"This is Thrall 7 *calling* Bard. *David, Sean, please—"*

David jammed open the comm before Mari finished her sentence. "Mari, it's David. Are you okay? I can't get any vid—"

She talked over him. *"David. I'm so happy to hear your voice. Dale is trying to sell me."* Her voice sounded like she held back tears.

"Mari, are you okay?" David tried to interject, but the words rushed out of her mouth so fast he could barely understand them.

"Some guy on Sinder Isle wants to cut my eyes out. So I destroyed the camera and got out of that horrible room. Carlos is dead, but not because of the battery. I couldn't help it. He destroyed the lock controls. I didn't know, David. I swear I didn't know."

Soli gasped, and David's heart pounded as he ignored the fear in Mari's voice so he could piece together her situation.

"Mari." He spoke calmly, as though they were sitting across from one another at dinner, like that night at the Rose of Sharon.

As she kept talking about becoming lost in the commonways, he tried again. "Mari." She quieted.

"Are you alone on the bridge right now?" he asked.

"Yes. I knocked out the nav leader."

"Did you lock yourself in?" Sean asked.

"Yes."

"Good," David said. "Now why are there alarms going off in the background?"

"Maybe because I vented the hydroponics bay. But I didn't have a choice." The panic swam in her voice again.

Sean swore under his breath.

Like David, he was probably imagining every horrific scenario. "It's okay, Mari. Is the ship still venting atmosphere?"

"No, the barrier sealed off that compartment."

Something was amiss. "The alarms should have cut out by now if the danger were contained. Look at your atmo readings for the entire ship. Is there another breach somewhere?"

"Let me see…no, they're reporting every place else as secure."

He was about to insist about the alarms, when Mari must have caught on.

"Wait. The alarms haven't stopped because I had to blow the failsafe on the condensers in the hydroponics bay. It's just the result of my bad rewiring."

He shot a look at Sean to see if that could be a real possibility. When Sean gave him a response somewhere between a nod and a shrug, David felt placated enough to return to his original question. "How about you? Are you okay?"

She didn't answer right away.

David suspected what that hesitation meant. And he knew she was keeping the truth from him when she answered, *"I'm okay."*

The thought of Dale or Carlos or any man raising his hand to Mari made David's blood boil. "Where is Dale now?"

"Probably headed here to the bridge."

"He can override the lock," Sean said.

Though he looked at David when he spoke, Mari responded.

"He can't. I destroyed the lock panel on this side. That should do it, right?"

"Probably," Sean said.

There were too many *probablys* in this whole scenario for David. He needed some concrete action. "Do you have full control of navigation, Mari?"

"Yes."

"Then you need to reroute to a public dock."

"Which one?"

Sean already had the information up on a screen in the holo-controls. "If she's headed toward Sinder Isle, then Abigail Landing is her best bet. It's a small municipal dock, but it's close enough that the reroute will be simple, plus the local contractors' guild is within a few kilometers."

"Hang on. Sean's sending you the coordinates for Abigail Landing."

David waited.

"Got them."

"Good. Let the auto-pilot make most of the adjustments for now. It will be too difficult to free-fly a ship as big as the *Thrall*. Your inertia alone will be fighting against you. That freighter won't maneuver like the *Bard,* but the principles are the same. It's the landing that's going to be touchy."

"I have to land this thing? By myself?" Her voice pitched higher in rising panic.

"I'll guide you when the time comes," David said. "This will be easy for you. I've never met anyone who could take to navigating and piloting like you, and that includes most of the fleet recruits I trained. You're smart, Mari. Maybe the smartest person that I know. All you have to do is remain calm and we'll do this together."

She offered silence in reply. David and Sean shared a concerned look. If Mari couldn't hold it together, they might lose her. Then a loud exhale sputtered through the comm, and Mari launched into a systems check with the confidence of a seasoned pilot.

"Navigation is go. Life support, go. Comms systems…except video, go. Auto systems are a go."

David grinned, and Sean actually gave him a half-smile in return.

She finished with, *"Systems check complete. I'm go on all systems."*

"Now reroute your arrival to Abigail Landing," David said.

"Rerouting."

They waited.

"Reroute confirmed."

"How close are you to re-entry protocol?" David asked.

"Looks like fifteen minutes."

"Good. Check your harness one last time." Every muscle in David's body was tense, but he had faith in Mari. He meant it when he said she was a natural at piloting.

"Hmm."

"What is it?" David asked.

"There's another transmission coming in."

"From Abigail Landing?" It made sense that the dock would be pitching a fit about an unscheduled freighter knocking at their door.

"Can't be," Sean said. "I've been trying to raise them the whole time to give them a warning, but haven't gotten through."

"It's from an Armadan gunship."

David's heart sped up and his mouth went dry. If the dock felt the *Thrall* was a threat, they'd call in the Armada. His mind went to the destruction of that UTV over Tampa One a year ago when he'd been ordered to take out the threat.

"Mari, open a channel to Abigail Landing and the gunship, then say this exactly. 'Armadan gunship, this is *Thrall 7* requesting an emergency docking at Abigail Landing. I am an unarmed civilian pilot.' Did you get all of that, Mari?"

"Yes."

The small affirmative was all he got before his comm link went silent.

"She'll get it right," Sean said, as though to affirm it to himself as much as to David.

David agreed, but said nothing in the tense silence.

"David, the gunship has a message for you."

"For me?" Had he heard her right?

"Yes, but I'm not going to repeat it because it's not very nice. Something about this serves you right for picking them so young. What does that mean?" Mari's tone hinted that she already understood the implication.

Sean snickered.

Relief flooded over any irritation or embarrassment David might have felt. "That means when you land, you get to meet my brother, Ben."

"The one who annoys the shit out of you?"

For the first time since this whole ordeal began, the mood lifted with tentative relief.

"That would be the one," David said.

"I like him already," Sean said.

"You haven't met him yet," David said.

A muffled explosion ripped through the comm, crashing the mood.

"Mari, what's happening?"

"Dale just blew the door to the brid—"

The comm went dead.

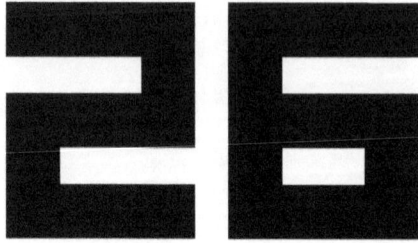

Mari screamed as the explosive wave rippled through the bridge, making her ears ring. The acrid odor of fried circuitry and melted plastic punctuated the detonation. She swiveled in the nav chair, the holo-orb rotating with her. Through the transparent glow of its orange and pink controls, she spied the damaged door. It had only opened a few centimeters, but bulged at its center from the blast. This warping would make a forced manual opening impossible. Dale still shoved against the twisted metal with both hands, but he would need a lot more muscle to move it. Several other hands joined his.

He pushed them away with a crazed shriek and managed to squeeze his left arm through the opening. As though under a spell, Mari simply stared at his contorted body trying to push past the equally twisted metal door. He was shoving his left leg in when he stopped to look at her. She could only see one crazed green eye and part of his mouth.

In between labored breaths he said, "When I get in there, I'm going to fucking kill you."

Then the comm blasted back on, so distorted Mari couldn't tell if it was David or someone else on the other end.

"David?"

Nothing coherent, just white noise.

To adjust the comm, her fingers flew over the airscreen inside the holo-controls, blurring her view of Dale's struggle with the bridge door.

A new alert bleated within the din of the breach alarm and sizzling comm. The ship took on a steeper angle and a slight pull of Gs tightened around Mari's skin.

Several thumps and curses came from the door area as Dale's men slammed into each other and into him, crushing him within the confines of the door.

She recognized the fear on his face as he also realized what was happening—the *Thrall 7* was initiating atmospheric reentry.

In a dizzying whirl of holo-controls, she spun the chair back to face the viewscreen. Tampa Deux's marble of blue and white filled her vision.

Reentry was the most critical part of a flight. The last thing Mari needed now was a crazy man distracting her. The auto-pilot had committed them, but perhaps the *Thrall* could save her from Dale, too. Her finger hovered above the little black button which would override the auto-pilot and return manual flight to her.

"Just press it." If no one else was around to encourage her, she'd have to depend on herself, something she'd been doing since last year.

She pressed the button.

The entire orb of holo-controls flashed an angry red, warning her that manual flight had been engaged.

She had expected the ship to buck or list or start spinning into the awaiting planet. But nothing felt different. Somehow that seemed unnerving, as though any second the whole ship would shudder and break apart.

"Don't invite misfortune." She murmured the phrase her mother always used. Growing up on Deleine Mari had always felt that someone must have invited a shipload of misfortune onto her family.

As if on cue, a flashing message alerted her that the angle of trajectory was slipping away from forty degrees and their speed was picking up. She felt the extra Gs press her back farther into the sour-smelling pilot's chair until she had to pant for shallow breaths.

She evened out the angle and velocity by making little adjustments with fingertip controls built into the nav chair. Thankfully someone had thought of this design perk, though someone who had probably never dreamt up her current scenario.

She heard clambering and cries behind her but couldn't lose focus as she put the *Thrall*'s hull shields against the burning and rumbling atmosphere of Tampa Deux. Waves of flame roiled past the viewscreen. She swore she could feel its heat as sweat formed along her brow and wet her palms. The light was beautiful, but so brilliant she could barely look at it. She probably should have put the outer shield down, but with Dale moving in, she had had to act fast.

Her approach was like a woozy bird, so she corrected, actually overcorrected. Doubt took root in her mind. She was in over her head. What if she crashed them?

The thought brought a rush of adrenaline, but not out of fear, out of an epiphany. That's how she'd take care of Dale upon landing—she'd crash the *Thrall*. Just a little bit.

Once they broke through the atmosphere, she edged their nose down a bit, sending new alarms blaring through the cabin and warnings flashing across the holo-controls. There were so many now her brain just ignored their pleas.

The *Thrall*'s auto-pilot kept kicking in, trying to level out the ship and engage airbrakes, but Mari kept enacting the override. She felt faint, either from the pressure or the stress. Maybe a little of both.

The altimeter counted down at a sickening pace, and the ground enlarged like zooming in on a vid screen. Mari suddenly thought this was a terrible idea—her heart pounded, she fought for breath that wasn't there. The silver grey docks of Abigail Landing filled her viewscreen. She squeezed her eyes shut just before impact because she was afraid to see her own death.

"Get a call out for an extra medical team…what's happening on the other decks… the ones still alive should be taken into custody…search for survivors on the bridge…."

Mari heard a man's voice fading in and out. Then she realized it was she who was fading in and out. Trying to force consciousness back with a deep breath, she only managed to choke.

"I'm here," she croaked out.

After another coughing fit, she called again. "Here!"

Dust thrown up from the crash stung at her lungs. Or was that smoke? The smell of scorched plastic and the snap and pop of circuitry, which burned outside her vision, gave her the answer.

A man in blue fatigues, a grey t-shirt, and navy flak jacket stepped through the settling smoke. He lowered his battle rifle and slung it into his shoulder harness as he picked his way over debris to get to her position.

This trooper looked so much like David in the eyes that Mari couldn't help but stare. His hair was much shorter, the military cut emphasizing his forehead, but the shock of rich brown was thick like David's. This guy's jaw wasn't quite as squared, but he certainly had the same build and bearing.

"You're Ben, aren't you?"

He crouched down next to her. "And you're the woman who's been kissing my brother."

Her surprise had to show on her face, as the blush that crawled down her cheeks and neck…past all the dirt and grime. She pulled at the harness trapping her in the nav chair, but Ben placed a halting hand on her arm. "Let's wait until I get my medic over here to be sure you're not injured, okay? You did just crash a freighter."

Ben's Yurian accent was stronger than David's, and his voice had a slightly richer tone. "Hans, over here," he yelled toward the back of the bridge.

She closed her eyes and wished it were David's hand on her arm. As the adrenaline seeped out of her body, she felt weary and distracted.

"Mari?"

Her eyes flew open at the sound of her name.

"It *is* Mari, right?" Ben asked, rubbing her arm.

She shook her head yes.

"I want to see those pretty eyes open, okay? We need to make sure you don't have a concussion."

Just then a dark-haired man with olive skin, who could have been mistaken for a contractor if not for his hazel eyes, introduced himself as Hans. Ben made to leave, but Mari snagged his hand. She didn't want to be alone anymore. Ben was the closest she could get to David right now, and that gave her comfort.

Ben whispered something to a female trooper near him, then stooped down and held Mari's hand with both of his. "Did David teach you how to fly?" he asked.

"Yeah." She smiled a little.

"I can tell he taught you how to land, too. This is just how his first flight ended." She and Hans both laughed.

"He must have gotten much better at landings by the time I served under him on the *Protector*," Hans said.

"David was your captain?" Mari asked.

"Yes. He was a good captain. I respect him for how he handled his command. A lot of us do. He's missed." Hans checked her pupil dilation with a small light.

Until now Mari hadn't thought of all the troopers who must know David, or know of him, because he was their commanding officer. It made her proud. "He's pretty great," she said.

"Yeah, yeah, I've heard that my entire life." Ben smiled like she'd seen David do so many times. "But I can tell you some stories from when we were kids that will make him seem a little more human."

"Like how you bit him and left that scar."

Ben laughed heartily. "I forgot about that. I'm surprised he fessed up to it instead of saying it was a battle scar."

"He showed me his battle scars, too."

"I have no doubt he did," Ben said.

Hans cleared his throat and tried to hide the smile on his face. "You're good to go. Just some lacerations and bruising, but you're going to be sore and stiff for a while."

"That just means David won't be showing you his scars any time soon," Ben said.

"Uh," Hans stood up and shifted uncomfortably. "If you don't need me here anymore, sir, I'll check on the prisoner."

Mari sobered, remembering the man who had put her in this situation to begin with. "What's going to happen to Dale?"

Ben worked on the straps holding Mari into the pilot's chair. "He'll be remanded into custody. The question right now is whether into ours or the local contractors' guild."

She heard a groan from the other side of the bridge as two troopers secured Dale on a stretcher.

Even after what he had done to her, Mari felt sick knowing it was her actions that had broken Dale's body. Then she remembered Carlos as though a dam to her memory had burst. She choked back a sob.

Ben maneuvered his body into her sight line so she couldn't see Dale as they removed him from the bridge. She found his eyes and whispered, "I killed Carlos. I blew out the hydroponics bay…." she choked on a sob. "And he was inside."

Ben was silent as he unsnapped the harness around her waist. He slid the shoulder straps down her bruised arms and whispered back, "You didn't kill anyone."

She looked at him in shock. "Did Carlos—"

"Carlos was the victim of an unfortunate accident. In your attempt to escape you had no idea that there would be a breach in the hydroponics bay. Let alone that Carlos would be inside it when that happened."

"But I—"

"Mari." Ben touched a hand under her chin and all she saw were David's eyes, eyes she trusted. "The record will show what happened in the hydroponics bay was an accident. Dale shouldn't have cut corners." Ben tried to smile, but it twisted into an angry set of his jaw with his next words. "And the son of a bitch shouldn't have abducted young women to sell to a psychopath. Carlos was part of that. He chose his fate. Don't ever doubt it."

Ben's conviction calmed Mari and allowed her to remember the abuse she had endured at Carlos's hands.

A female trooper with sculpted cheekbones that Mari envied interrupted their conversation. "Lieutenant Anlow, we got a call from the Embassy. We're to turn over Zapona and his crew to the contractors working Abigail Landing."

Ben shot to his feet. "Bullshit. This is a fleet issue. Who the hell gave this order?"

"Rainer Varden, the Sovereign's Head Contractor, and he claims that it's not our jurisdiction because the freighter has permission to cross planetary lines."

"Dale Zapona was transporting an abducted person against her will. That's all the jurisdiction we fucking need. Plus this guy is wanted for questioning in an Armadan matter. Get Varden back on the comm. I want to talk to this idiot."

"Are they going to let Dale go?" Mari asked.

Ben stopped his ranting at the sound of her small voice. He smiled David's calming smile. "It will be okay." But just like his older brother, the anger burning behind Ben's eyes said something different.

She took a deep breath and attempted to get out of the nav chair, but the angle was awkward.

Ben caught her as she tumbled over. And before she could help herself she was hugging him tight and crying.

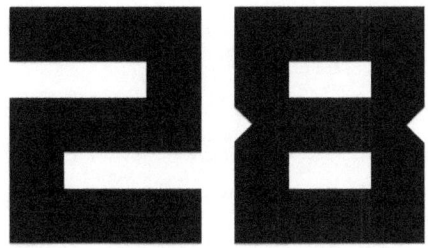

When worlds collide.

Seeing Ben escort Mari out of an Armadan gunship was one of the most surreal sights David could have imagined. Even with an oversized jacket in fleet blue draped over her shoulders and buckled up black combat boots, Mari's vibrancy contrasted sharply against the stolid grey of the ship.

For this one single instant, here on the only dock not cordoned off at Abigail Landing, David's past and future meshed as the sun drew pink rays along the clouds on its way over the horizon. Under different circumstances he might have appreciated the whimsy. But there was nothing light-hearted about how they had all come to this moment—at the hands of some privileged asshole who was free to mess with other people's lives due to some kind of bullshit Embassy cover up.

When Ben first told David that Dale would probably walk, that the contractors in charge of the investigation didn't even bother to take Mari's statement, David hadn't said a word. Ben said enough for both of them, used every last filthy epithet he could dig up to describe the injustice. Not that it made either of them feel any better.

David held back as the rest of the *Bard*'s passengers welcomed Mari home amidst the organized chaos of fleet soldiers, medical teams, and contractors milling about. Mari had done a pretty good job with the landing, only causing damage to one end of the narrow dock. When Ben had first told him Mari crashed on purpose, David was stunned, but he hadn't been there, hadn't gone through what she went through, so wouldn't judge how she handled it. She was alive. It was all that mattered to him.

Ben rubbed Mari's shoulder and stooped over to whisper in her ear before leaving her to Soli and Sean. David could tell by the rigidity of Ben's posture as he walked toward him that his brother was still pissed by the bureaucratic slap in the face they had all received.

Soli was the first to embrace Mari, no doubt using the ship's external cameras to record the event. David tried not to feel harshly about what he considered an intrusion upon this private moment. Soli had a duty to record events like this for the archives whether David liked it or not.

When Sean gave Mari a big hug and kissed her on the cheek, she laughed. David smiled. He could finally see their interaction the way Sean saw it—as an older brother taking care of his little sister. There was still a small part of David that kept a slight jealousy in check, though, because Mari and Sean would always have a history that began well before David ever met her.

"She's a tough little thing," Ben said as he approached.

"Yeah," David said. "Don't let the short skirt fool you."

"I'm surprised you're not over there, ripping her out of that guy's arms," Ben said.

"You know I'm not the jealous type."

"Bull fucking shit."

David threw an arm around Ben's shoulders and drew him into a quick hug. He gave his brother a kiss on top of the head before letting him go. "Thank you. For bringing her back to me."

"Wish I could have brought back a little justice, too."

"They're really not going to charge Dale?"

Ben's dark look said it all. "He was remanded into contractor custody and will supposedly be questioned during his recovery."

"And Stavros?"

"Nothing implicating him, short of Dale Zapona going on a live Media feed and telling the entire system what that fucker's been doing," Ben said. "But even then, the Embassy would find a way out for Stavros. Wish I would have questioned Dale before I turned him over. I guarantee we'd have a confession and at least enough dirt on Stavros to petition a fleet investigation."

David hadn't forgotten that Stavros was not only responsible for Mari's abduction, but also for the deaths of several good troopers.

"Oh, you never know. Maybe you'll have a shot at Dale one day," David said.

Ben said something in return, but David's attention drifted back to Mari, who was alone now that Sean and Soli walked back onto the *Bard*. The warmth of her smile went straight through his chest. He'd missed that feeling. Leaving Ben in mid-sentence, David covered the distance to her in a few strides.

"Hi." Her voice sounded strained.

He pulled her into a gentle hug, almost afraid that if he greeted her the way he wanted to, he'd break her. "Mari." Her name was all he could manage as emotion took his voice. He kept rubbing her back and smoothing her hair as he fought for control. His hands actually shook, like a man recovering from shock.

When she relaxed into his embrace and said, "I missed you," he let the relief flood through him.

He drew her face up to him and kissed her like it was their first kiss all over again, only this time it meant something much more. He could tell by the way she returned his intimacy that she knew it, too.

When they finally pulled apart, David stared into those gorgeous eyes for a moment, then said, "From now on, when you leave the ship, I'm coming with you."

She laughed at his joke, not realizing that he mostly meant it.

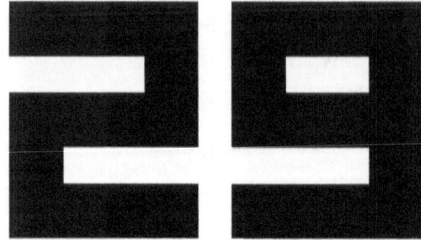

"Sorry about tonight," Mari said.

She and David were nestled on one of the plush mauve couches in the *Bard*'s lounge and staring out the windows at the lights of the Hub from their usual berth space. The scene was calming. At least from inside the ship.

"I'm happy staying in." David nuzzled her in his lap.

She melted into his chest, relaxing in his scent.

Everyone else, even Sean, had gone out for the evening, but Mari wasn't in the mood to leave this time. Right now she just needed to look at the world from afar. And the glittering activity of Shiraz Dock and Carrey Bay provided a pretty nice view.

"We'll be back here in another two weeks to get our new passenger anyway," David said. "I think she's your age. And Sean's already not happy about her coming on board so that should be entertaining for a while." David squeezed her knee playfully.

"Yeah, that will be fun." Her voice didn't portray much enthusiasm. Even a week after her abduction, the memories still haunted her.

Her experience left her feeling triumphant in many ways because she had survived. Not just survived—she'd taken control out of her captors' hands and made her escape, commanded the situation. But it had left its scars.

David inadvertently reminded her of the physical ones as he slid his fingertips over her arms where the mender patches had healed her bruises. The darkness behind his eyes when he had first seen the other Armadan's fingerprints imbedded in her skin was chilling.

When she confessed how Carlos had met his death, he assured her it wasn't her fault, that no matter what, Carlos deserved to die for his part in her abduction and the countless other women who hadn't gotten away. She believed David was right, but she still saw Carlos's face every once in a while when she closed her eyes. David called it post-traumatic stress and said he'd helped his soldiers deal with it before. She suspected he'd had to deal with it himself as well, though he was still rather close-lipped about his fleet time.

That didn't bother her anymore. He'd share everything when the time was right. Like he'd said, they had forever. She interlaced her fingers with his, enjoying the warmth of his touch. A stirring of desire passed through her body, the first since her return. They hadn't been intimate again yet, but David slept next to her every night because she asked him to. It made her feel safe...well, *safer*.

She twisted in his arms to face him. "I'm afraid Dale will come back."

Not until this moment had she spoken these words out loud, but the thought had consumed her, bringing on panic attacks that she tried to hide from the others. David could always tell when she was upset, though. And he was always there to comfort her. His gentle affection never wavered.

"He's not coming back."

"But they let him go."

He stroked her hair as though considering his next words. "The charges may have been dropped, but I promise you that Dale is *never* coming back. And I will always keep my promises to you."

The conviction in his eyes made her believe it. She kissed him and it felt good. Now all they needed were fireworks over the water.

Did he really think he'd get away with what he did?

David cut the razor wire crowning the wall outside Dale's estate.

"If this goes well," Ben said. "I'll be incommunicado for a while."

Ben didn't need to say more. He and his team disappeared on covert operations pretty often, once for an entire year. But this time it would be personal. Ben would make sure Liu Stavros paid for all the Armadan lives he took.

"Thanks for this, Ben."

His brother slapped him on the shoulder and grinned—Ben smiled more than any soldier David had ever known.

Ben clicked an all-go signal to his team through his reporter before he and David dropped over the side of the wall. Their boots smashed into a bed of calla lilies with blooms folded and drooping now that the sun had gone down over Wright's Landing.

Every footfall shattered the garden's perfection, each squashed stem and dislodged petal adding to the defacement. The brothers moved silently through the proud grounds, leaving a trail of crushed beauty in their wake.

David held up his hand for Ben to stop.

There it was. The hole in Dale's defenses—quite literally a hole in the wall.

David had noticed this scarecrow when he and Mari first strolled through the garden. Had he not seen a butterfly attempt to land on the stone, only to flutter straight through it, as though disappearing into the wall itself, he wouldn't have detected this secret entrance to the house.

"This the spot?" Ben whispered.

"Yeah, and it's probably mined as well as alarmed."

"Alarm's down, according to my team. They didn't detect any mines, but I'll let you go first, just to be sure." Ben flashed his smile.

David knew better. Ben would lay down his life for his family, both blood relatives and those bonded to him by the call of duty. With a nod of understanding, David unsheathed his knife and tossed it through the holographic piece of wall. They each took cover to either side of the implied opening and shielded their faces.

Nothing. No explosive mines, no blaring alarms.

"Your team's good," David said.

"The best," Ben agreed.

They walked right out of Dale's garden and through the scarecrow, ignoring the cameras hovering low in the sky around them. Ben's team had done their job and rerouted the video feed and sensors on Dale's security system. If they worked this the right way, tonight would be a two-for-one, each Anlow brother getting his own retribution.

David stayed low, Ben following closely behind him. They ran among the finely manicured flowerbeds, trampling delicate blooms and wispy stems with their combat boots. The pungent scent of marigolds mixed with freshly trod zinnias and nearby rose bushes. They stayed away from the central paths to avoid walking in the open and the crunch of pea gravel underfoot. David and Ben waded through thigh-high peonies, their scarlet and purple petals folded in on themselves. Feeling exposed, David picked up his pace the last few meters to the iron gate.

He pulled the borrowed battle rifle off his shoulder and used its night scope to check out the veranda beyond the gate. Satisfied, he gave the all-clear signal to Ben. Single file they crept onto the wide, covered patio, sweeping around huge planters bulging with foliage and flowers whose colors were muted by the scant light of night. They snaked around tables and chairs of elegant metal craftsmanship, keeping as far away from the house as possible.

Heavy curtains held the golden interior light at bay, but the possibility remained for them to cast shadows. David put up his hand for another halt as they came to a set of glass doors, also curtained. But no lights shone out of this room. David switched his scope to infrared. One heat signature inside, prone as though lying on its side. He looked to Ben for confirmation. Ben glanced at his palm screen and nodded his head in an affirmative. The tracker showed that Dale Zapona waited on the other side of the glass.

David checked the door. The handle turned without resistance. Another fine job by Ben's tech team.

Keeping the night scope up to his right eye, David placed one foot after the other to move soundlessly over the thick carpet. Dale lay on his side, facing David. With the muzzle of his rifle he jabbed Dale in the forehead. Dale woke up with a start, but David kept him pinned with the weapon and forced him on his back.

"Who are you? How did you get in here?"

David had the advantage because Dale couldn't see in the dark. Through the green-white artificial light of the scope, David studied the last remnants of Dale's wounds from the crash. In another week they'd be gone, but the scars he'd left in Mari's mind would stay with her a lot longer. David swallowed his anger. They were here for answers.

"Where do I find Liu Stavros?" he asked.

Dale's expression changed, as though David's voice sparked some subtle recognition. Part of him hoped it did, though keeping Dale off-balance was better for their plan.

"I don't know who that is." Dale's voice took on a haughty tone.

David ground the hard steel of the muzzle into the soft flesh of Dale's brow. He felt like smashing it right through his skull, but they needed information.

"You're crazy if you think I'm telling you anything."

David increased the pressure of the muzzle, drawing a gasp of aggravated pain from Dale.

"My security force—"

"Was already taken care of," David said. "I guess Carlos wasn't so easy to replace. Sorry to hear he got sucked out into space like half of your freighter."

Dale's protests stopped upon hearing that bit of news.

Part of the effectiveness for on-site interrogations like this was stripping the target of all feelings of security. The simple idea that Dale was no longer safe in his own home should weaken his resolve, mess with his equilibrium, make him more likely to talk in his confused state. Hinting that his captor knew details about Dale's recent incident that even the Media hadn't reported had the added effect.

"Do I know you?" Dale asked, fear replacing his earlier bravado.

Yeah, you do, you piece of shit.

"Where do I find Liu Stavros?"

"I told you I don't know who that is."

The panic was starting to rise, but right now Dale was more afraid of Stavros than the threat of a battle rifle.

"We know you do," David said.

"We?" Dale's eyes rolled around in his sockets as though that would help him penetrate the shadows and outlines of the black room. That sensory deprivation did part of their work, making the man's imagination work over time.

"You've got more than one gun trained on you right now," Ben said from the other side of the bed.

David slid his battle rifle into the side holster to free his hands. He forced Dale's arm away from his body. Snatching a short blade from his thigh sheath, David stabbed the knife through Dale's palm, pinning him to the bed. Dale cried out and tried to grab at the hilt, but David had a second blade out and jammed into Dale's shoulder, rendering that arm immobile, as well.

Dale shrieked.

"I have more of those. You make me draw the next one and I'm cutting your hand off to get to your reporter. That's the only problem with your fancy implanted kind, you can't just take it off."

Dale's screams died out into a whimper.

"It might take us a while to decode and trace any recent communications you had with Stavros," David continued, "but we'll eventually get it. You can save us some time and save your hand by giving up his location to us right now."

Dale opened his mouth to scream again, but David pressed the edge of another knife against Dale's cheek as a deterrent. "Are you going to take the simple way out?"

Dale's speech came out in a sputter. "Stavros is on Sinder Isle."

"Wrong answer," Ben called out. "We were already there. Looks like he left for a little holiday."

"Where do we find him?" David slid the knife along a freshly healed piece of new pink skin. Dale whimpered, tears streaking down his face.

It just made David want to cut him more. "Where?"

"Noveopini Territory on Tampa Three," Dale blurted. "But he'll be under an alias."

"Which would be?" David pressed.

Dale hesitated until David whipped the blade from his cheek and sliced a chunk out of Dale's ear.

"Mario Buhl," he said through gritted teeth.

"I have the team checking it out now," Ben said.

"You won't find anything in the Embassy files about him," Dale said.

"So, you're saying we just have to take your word for it?" David asked.

Alarms blared inside and outside.

"Time to wrap it up," Ben said.

"That just cost you a hand," David said.

With one clean cut, David severed Dale's wrist from his arm and threw the appendage to Ben. Dale's screams filled the room as he thrashed the stub of his arm around. "Please don't kill me. I'll give you anything you want…money, girls. I can get you women, any kind you want."

David moved away from Dale and flipped on a bedside lamp.

When Dale's gaze met David's and he was sure there was recognition lighting the panicked expression, David snapped his battle rifle around and fixed it on Dale.

"I wanted you to know it was me. You should have never taken her from me, Dale." David fired two fast projectile rounds into the middle of Dale's forehead.

Promise kept.

THE PLANETS OF
THE AMBASADORA-VERSE

TAMPA ONE

The first to be terraformed, Tampa One was only halfway settled before its larger neighbor, Tampa Deux, was ready for habitation. Home to large swaths of unspoiled wilderness, like Archenzon, much of the planet remains a preserve for millions of species of animal and plant life.

TAMPA DEUX

Heavily populated, even after Tampa Three was terraformed, Tampa Deux's popularity still grows because of its infrastructure and planning.

TAMPA THREE

The smallest of all the planets, it was originally meant to be an exclusive world for Socialite families with the most money; however, bad terraforming and rushed planning made this the least desirable location in the system.

YURAI

This world was terraformed to compete with Tampa Three as the optimal planet. Socialites left it to the Armadans because they believed its potential wasn't as high as Tampa Three, but now Yurai's size and wealth is rivaled only by Tampa Quad.

TAMPA QUAD

The most populated planet in the system, Tampa Quad is the center of government and commerce. As the largest planet, Tampa Quad boasts more inhabitants per square foot than any other, while still maintaining as much wild space as Tampa One.

DELEINE

Deleine was the newest to be terraformed, mainly so that workers could be close to the plethora of uranium, iridium, and boxite mines there. The extensive mining has caused health issues, especially among the less genetically diverse Socialites.

About the Author

Heidi Ruby Miller uses research for her stories as an excuse to roam the globe. With degrees in Anthropology, Geography, Foreign Languages, and Writing, she knew early that penning fast-paced, exotic adventures would be her life.

She's put her experiences and studies to paper in her far-future *Ambasadora* series and into *Atomic Zion*, the beginning of her new supernatural spy series.

In between trips, Heidi teaches creative writing at Seton Hill University, where she graduated from their renowned Writing Popular Fiction Graduate Program the same month she appeared on Who Wants To Be A Millionaire. *Ambasadora* was her thesis novel there, and the multi-award winning writing guide *Many Genres, One Craft*, which she co-edited with Michael A. Arnzen, is based on the Seton Hill program and was named #5 in The Writer magazine's Ten Most Terrific Writing Books of 2011.

She has had various fiction and non-fiction publications, as well as various jobs, including contract archaeologist, foreign currency exchanger at Walt Disney World, foreign language teacher, and educational marketing director for a Frank Lloyd Wright house. Currently she is an editor at Dog Star Books and sometimes co-hosts author interviews on the GoingLIVE talk show on FCTV.

Heidi is a member of The Authors Guild, International Thriller Writers, Pennwriters, Broad Universe, SFR Brigade, and Science Fiction Poetry Association.

She's fond of high-heeled shoes, action movies, Chanel, and tea of any sort. You can read about her books, travels, and author interviews at http://heidirubymiller.blogspot.com and tweet her @heidirubymiller.

She lives near Pittsburgh with her traveling companion and writer husband, Jason Jack Miller.

Contact her at heidirubymiller@gmail.com.

www.ingramcontent.com/pod-product-compliance
Lightning Source LLC
Chambersburg PA
CBHW050907180626
46814CB00007B/2936